Basil C. Thomson

Savage Island

Outlook

Basil C. Thomson

Savage Island

1. Auflage | ISBN: 978-3-73263-006-6

Erscheinungsort: Frankfurt am Main, Deutschland

Erscheinungsjahr: 2018

Outlook Verlag GmbH, Frankfurt.

SAVAGE ISLAND

BY THE SAME AUTHOR

SAVAGE ISLAND

AN ACCOUNT OF A SOJOURN
IN NIUÉ AND TONGA

By BASIL C. THOMSON

LONDON
JOHN MURRAY, ALBEMARLE STREET
1902

PREFACE

NIUÉ, more commonly known as Savage Island, lies 1,000 miles N.N.E. of New Zealand, and 300 miles S.S.E. of Samoa, in the loneliest spot in that part of the Pacific. Its iron-bound coasts tempt no vessels to call for supplies. At rare intervals great four-masted timber-ships pass in the offing; more rarely still schooners call to replenish the stock of the traders and to carry away their copra.

I went to the Niuéans in the name of the Queen and Empress whom the world is still lamenting, and I do not like to think of what our loss means to the people in these remote outposts of her Empire. The oldest native in the South Seas remembers no sovereign's name but hers. She was a real person to them all; a lady who had made them her especial care, had sent the gospel to them, and had bade them lay aside their clubs, and live in peace, order, and equity. Vika, as they called her affectionately—Vika, after whom they named their girl-children—was the benign, all-powerful chief, whose house was built upon the coral strand of Lonitoni (London), opposite the landing-place, where her men-o'-war were moored stem and stern in rows before her door. She read their letters with her own eyes, and had her captains to sit before her on the floor-mats while she gave them messages for the brown folk in far islands. And now Vika, the well-beloved, has left them, mourned by the empire of which they were but the tiniest part. It was hers, and she never saw it; but we, who have seen it—who have, in the humblest way, helped in the making of it
—think with heavy hearts of how much hangs upon a name, and of how hard it will be to reassure them, when, as they say of their own dead kings, "kuo hala 'ae langi"—"the heaven has fallen."

NORTHAMPTON, 1901

SAVAGE ISLAND

CHAPTER I

THE ISLAND AND ITS PEOPLE

"TO Her Majesty Queen Victoria, Queen of Great Britain, the first kingdom of all the kingdoms of the world.

"We the chiefs and rulers and governors of Niué-Fekai desire to pray Your Majesty, if it be your pleasure, to stretch out towards us your mighty hand, that Niué may hide herself in it and be safe. We are afraid lest some other powerful nation should come and trouble us, and take possession of our island, as some islands in this quarter of the world have been taken by great nations. On account of this we are troubled, but we leave it with you to do as seems best to you. If you send the flag of Britain, it is well; or if you send a Commissioner to reside among us, that also will be well.

"Our king, Tuitonga, died on the 13th July last, but before he died he wished to write to Your Majesty, and beg you to send the powerful flag of Britain to unfurl in this island of Niué, in order that this weak island of ours might be strong. It was from your country that men first came to this island to make known the name of the Lord, and through them this land of Niué-Fekai became enlightened; then, for the first time, this people knew that there were other lands in the world. Therefore the people of this land rejoice in you and in your kingdom. This land is enlightened by the gospel of Jesus Christ brought by the subjects of Your Majesty, and that is why we make this petition.

"That is all we have to say. May Your Majesty the Queen and your powerful kingdom be blessed, together with the kingdom of Niué, in the kingdom of Heaven.

"I, Fataäiki, write this letter."

Thus wrote Fataäiki, King of Niué, otherwise known as Savage Island, thirteen years ago.

The first request for a protectorate was made to a missionary as early as 1859, when the people were in the first heat of conversion to Christianity; this seems to have gone no further. But King Fataäiki's letter reached its destination, and England, "the first kingdom of all the kingdoms of the world," England the earth-hungry and insatiable (as others see her), took thirteen years to think it over, and then, having received a second letter more precisely worded, reluctantly consented. It is an object-lesson of the way in which we blunder into Empire.

It was not until the Germans began to develop their plantations in Samoa that Niué was discovered to have a value. The Polynesian races, as everybody knows, are a picturesque, easy-going, and leisure-loving people, too fond of home to travel, and too indolent to do a steady day's work. A dash of some alien blood, as yet unrecognised, has played strange freaks with the men of Niué. Alone among Polynesian races they opposed the landing of Europeans; alone they love to engage as labourers far from home, and show, both at home and abroad, a liking for hard work; no other island race has the commercial instinct so keenly developed. The number of them working in Samoa has increased so rapidly in recent years that their houses form a distinct quarter of the town of Apia, and when the recent troubles broke out they went in a body to the British Vice-Consul and claimed his protection as British subjects. It was hard to turn away people who were fellow-subjects by inclination, and to put the case at its lowest, our need of plantation labourers is tenfold greater than the Germans'. And so, when we had to receive from Germany an equivalent for the surrender of our claims in Samoa, Niué was thrown into our side of the scale in what is known as the "Samoa Convention, 1899," and it became my duty when negotiating a British protectorate over the independent kingdom of Tonga in 1900, to visit the island and announce a favourable answer to the petition forwarded thirteen years before.

So little was known of the lonely island that we approached it with mixed feelings—anxiety on the part of the captain, and high curiosity in those unconcerned with the navigation of the ship. There were, indeed, other feelings among our company, for we had been plunging into a strong headsea ever since we left the shelter of a Tongan harbour, and H.M.S. *Porpoise* has a reputation as a sea boat on which it would be charitable not to enlarge. The island has never been surveyed—indeed, the greater part of it is still indicated in the chart by a dotted line—and the brief paragraph devoted to it in the "Sailing Directions" is not encouraging to navigators. While the wind was in the east, a precarious anchorage might be found at more than one point on the western side, but let the wind shift to the west, and you were on a lee shore of precipitous cliffs.

As the grey cloud, that stretched like a bow across our course, grew in definition, the least sea-going of our party staggered to the deck. The island appeared to be what indeed it is—a coral reef upheaved from the sea-bed by some terrific convulsion—a Falcon Island of old time, only made of solid coral instead of pumice, and thirteen miles long instead of two furlongs. Not a hill nor a depression broke the monotonous line, but a fuzzy indistinctness in the drawing betokened that the place was densely wooded, as all limestone islands are. The sea was moderating; already we had begun to feel the influence of that great natural breakwater; with a strong glass we could make out a cluster of white houses nestling among the palm trees. Setting our course for them, we steamed in, until the sea grew calm and the steady breeze broke into sharp puffs with still air between. On either hand, as far as the eye could reach, the sea dashed against an abrupt limestone cliff, unprotected by any reef; here breaking into smoky spray that dimmed the far horizon, there thundering into inky caverns. A hundred feet above sprang the wall of dark green timber, broken here and there by clusters of cocoanut palms that shaded trim villages, with roofs of thatch and walls of dazzling white. Neatest of all was our haven of Alofi, for there the houses were fenced, and a grass lawn sloped down to the edge of the cliffs. Before the lead touched the bottom a fleet of small canoes had put out to meet us. Something unusual about these caught the eye; it was not the canoe, which was of the out-rigged build common to these seas; it was the crew. Every man wore a hat instead of a turban, and a sober coat and trousers instead of a bronze skin and a gay waist- cloth. From one of these— the only craf t that carried more than one man—a youth boarded us, and, introducing himself as Falani (Frank), the son of the late king, mounted the bridge, and offered to pilot us to an anchorage.

"SHIP AHOY!"

Our first visitors from Savage Island

"What you come here for?" he inquired, with an easy unconsciousness of his responsibilities towards the ship. "You come to hoist flag?" But his thoughts were elsewhere, for presently, espying the captain's black steward, he descended to the deck, and began to seek occasion for bringing himself under the notice of a functionary who, he had a right to assume, would have control of the proper perquisites of a pilot. Thereafter we saw little more of him. That a person of such exalted rank should volunteer his services as pilot to even the humblest ship proceeded, as we afterwards learned, from no public spirit; the only spirit that drew him forth from the shore was that which is kept in the steward's pantry. But for this frailty he might have succeeded his royal father, but he had now forfeited all his chances of succession by refusing to vacate the tin-roofed palace, built by public subscription as an official residence for future monarchs, on a site which, owing to an unfortunate oversight, was still the private property of the royal family. The reputation of the rightful heir requires no comment from me, if so commercially-minded a people could prefer the building of a second palace at Tuapa to being ruled over by the occupant of the original.

Some four hundred yards from the base of the cliff the lead gave nineteen fathoms, and there the anchor was let go. It caught upon the extreme edge of a submarine precipice, for soundings under the counter gave sixty-three fathoms; and if a westerly wind would put us on a lee shore, it was equally manifest that a strong easterly puff might set us dragging our anchor into deep water. We might have found better holding ground closer in, but it is not good to play tricks with His Majesty's ships, and as we had decided to keep the fires banked until our departure, there was nothing to be gained by moving. The captain may have had in his mind the case of another ship-of-war that anchored in seventeen fathoms in a secure but unsurveyed harbour for three days, when the navigating officer happened to notice that a blue-jacket, casting off one of the boats from the boom, was using his boat-hook as a punt pole against some object a few feet below the surface of the water. It was then discovered that all the ship's company, except the officers, were aware that the ship was anchored a few feet from a sharp-pointed rock, upon which any veer in the wind would have impaled her, but that no one had considered it his business to mention what it was the officers' duty to find out for themselves.

I lost no time in sending a boat ashore for Mr. Frank Lawes, the representative of the London Missionary Society, who, from his long residence and his kindly influence over the natives, has long been regarded by them as their adviser in all matters at issue between the Europeans and themselves, and who has so modestly and tactfully discharged the duties of his unsought office that Europeans and natives alike have cheerfully accepted his arbitration. He came on board at once, and willingly tendered his services, nominally as interpreter, but actually as a great deal more than that. He is a man of middle age, of gentle, sympathetic, and rather melancholy mien, with a vein of quiet humour, and a manner that would inspire confidence and affection in the native races of any country. He was anxious that we should move the ship to the king's village of Tuapa, for it seems that the key to native politics in Niué is the jealousy between village and village. To summon the headmen to the king's village could not be misinterpreted, but to send for the king to Alofi would be not only to put the old gentleman into ill-humour, but to imply a pre-eminence in Alofi that would in no wise be tolerated or forgiven by its fellow villages. But, since his description of Tuapa disclosed the fact that the anchorage was vile, and the landing-place such that it would probably be necessary to wade ashore in full-dress uniform, we decided to brave the royal displeasure, and to send a message explaining that a Queen's ship is not as other ships, and that although, out of consideration for her safety, our bodies must be landed at Alofi, our hearts would certainly be in that capital of capitals, Tuapa. Mr. Lawes, having taken upon himself the task of despatching messages to each of the eleven villages, inviting all the inhabitants of the island to a solemn council at ten o'clock the next morning, most kindly begged us to take up our quarters on shore with him, and took his leave.

There were, meanwhile, signs of a stir on shore. Men were running down to the landing-place with planks to build a wharf, and a fluttering crowd of women and children lined the edge of the cliff. When we reached the shore we wondered no longer that the Europeans in Niué prefer canoes to boats when they have to board a ship. There is a slit in the fringing reef of coral just wide enough to admit a boat, which heaves and falls with the swell in imminent peril of being ground to splinters against its jagged sides.[1] But there are no better boatmen in the world than the English blue-jackets, and in a few seconds we were hoisted upon the crazy pier with our baggage.

There was a smile of welcome on every native face, and we had a good opportunity for noting the characteristics of this interesting people. The men are generally shorter than the Samoans and Tongans, and their well-knit muscular bodies are less inclined to accumulate fat. Their features are smaller, and they often have a pinched appearance, as if they had originally been cast in a larger mould and compressed, like toy faces of india-rubber. Their colour is darker than the Samoan, and their bright eyes and vivacious gestures show that they have far greater energy and activity. Their hair is now cropped short, and very few wear beards, but this is a mark of civilisation, for the warriors of old depended upon hair and beard, plaited and ornamented with shells, and long enough to chew between their teeth, for striking terror into the hearts of their enemies. They all wore suits of European slop clothing, complete except for boots, and wide-brimmed hats plaited at home. The women wear the flowing *sacque*—a kind of nightgown of coloured print not taken in at the waist—like the women of Tahiti and Rarotonga. They had the same facial characteristics as the men, but they were fleshier in youth and more disposed to corpulence in age. They had long and rather coarse black hair, sometimes knotted on the back of the head, but more often hanging loose down the back. It is a pity that they do not follow the cleanly custom of Tonga and Fiji of smearing the hair with lime once a week, which, besides dyeing it a becoming auburn, serves other more practical purposes. That Niué is destitute of running water might be seen in a glance at their clothing, which has always to be washed with water in which soap will not lather. In a large assemblage such as this it was easy to recognise two distinct racial types—the one clearly Polynesian, the other doubtful. This admixture is an ethnological puzzle which I shall discuss later.

The Mission-house is a vast thatched building with walls of concrete, partitioned off into a number of large rooms, and standing in its own small compound. Most cool and spacious it seemed after the confined quarters in a third-class cruiser. The space before the verandah is planted with the flowering shrubs of which you may see dwarfed specimens in the tropical houses at Kew. I was surprised to find that this little compound was the only land on the island which Mr. Lawes could call his own. He could not even have milk, because when he kept a cow he was always having to meet claims by his parishioners for the damage it was alleged to have done. Judging by the ways of Missions in other parts of the Pacific, I may safely say that if any other than the London Missionary Society had taken Niué, it would have made the island a "Mission field" in the more literal sense. For itself it would have taken the eyes of the land; the pastor would have had a horse and a boat and a company of white-robed student servants to wait upon him; as in Hawaii and New Zealand, he would have acquired a handsome little landed property of his own, and for the natives there would have been left what the Mission had no use for. Here the missionary must pay for everything except the very rare presents of produce that are made him, and though four-fifths of the island are overgrown with bush, he has not land enough to keep a cow. I do not say which I think is the better system; I only contrast the two.

In the afternoon we were taken to see the cave of the Tongans. Public curiosity having now subsided, the village had resumed its normal appearance. It is cleaner and tidier even than it looked from the sea. The grass that stretches like a lawn to the cliff's edge, laced with the delicate shadow of the palm leaves, is bounded on the landward side by a stiff row of cottages, all built as exactly to plan as if a surveyor to a county council had had a hand in it, with lime-washed walls so dazzling that the eye lifts instinctively to the cool brown thatch to find rest. Every doorway is closed with a rough-hewn door; every window with broad, unpainted slats pivoted on the centre, so as to form a kind of fixed Venetian blind that admits the air and excludes the sun and rain—a device learned, it seems, from the Samoan teachers, who must in their turn have adapted it from the Venetian blinds of some European house in their own islands. These cottages are divided into rooms by thin partitions of wood or reeds that reach to the eaves, leaving the roof space open. Most of them are floored with palm-leaf matting, and a few boxes and wooden pillows are the only furniture. The cooking is done in little thatched huts in the rear. Mr. Lawes confessed that the older natives keep these cottages for show, preferring to live on week-days in the thatched hovels that contented their ancestors. You may see one of these behind each cottage, rickety when new, and growing year by year more ruinous until the crumbling rafters and rotten thatch are ripe for the firebrand that puts an end to their existence. Besides his town house, every householder has a building on his plantation in which he passes the nights during the planting and copra-making season with such of his family and friends as care to work with him. A thatched roof and frail wicker-work walls, with a mat or two to sleep on, and an iron pot for cooking, are all that he needs when the days from dawn to sunset are spent in hard work upon the land.

THE CHURCH AT ALOFI

A STREET IN ALOFI

It is curious to note how the native clings to the form, however he may vary the material, of his architecture. The Savage Island hut of Cook's time, with its rounded ends, took the shape of an elongated oval, and the concrete walls of the modern cottage are moulded to the same form. In Tonga, where corrugated iron, alas! is gradually usurping the place of thatch, the roof was rounded in the form of a scow turned bottom upwards, and the sheets of iron, with infinite skill and labour, have been tortured into the same form. The King of Tonga told me that it was hopeless to attempt to rebuild the fine native church built in 1893 by his great-grandfather in Vavau, and destroyed in the hurricane of April 2nd, because, although the posts and rafters were all intact, and had only to be cut loose from their lashings to be fit for use again, there was not a builder left in the group who understood the art of so lashing them in place as to produce the bellying curve which appeals to the Tongan eye for beauty in architecture. The new edifice, he said, must be built of weatherboard and iron.

The church in Niué, being simply a glorified native house, was an excellent object-lesson in the Polynesian system of building. The South Sea Island architect, whether Polynesian or Melanesian, thinks in fathoms, which he measures with the span of his outstretched arms, but whereas the Fijian is obliged to regulate the size of his house by the length of the *vesi* trunk he can find for his king posts, the Samoan and Tongan, by a more elaborate arrangement of his interior supports, may build a roof as lofty as he pleases. The ridge pole of the Fijian rests upon two uprights, buried for two-sevenths of their length in the ground if the house is to withstand hurricanes; and, since it is impossible to find straight *vesi* trunks more than fifty-four feet long, the ridge pole can never be more than forty-two feet above the ground. And since the sense of proportion would be wounded by a house being too long for its height, there is no public building in Fiji more than sixty-six feet long—the length of the great *bure* at Bau and the court house at Natuatuathoko (Fort Carnarvon). The system of supports for the Tongan roof-tree is best shown by a sectional diagram. By elongating the side and centre supports, such a building may be seventy or eighty feet high and of a proportionate length and breadth. If it succumbs to a hurricane, the roof merely slips from the supporting posts and subsides in a single piece, held firmly together by its sinnet lashings, as was the case with the great church at Vavau, shown in the illustration. Far otherwise is it with a weatherboard building overtaken by the same fate. The Government offices in Vavau were reduced to a mere heap of kindling wood, for lashings, by reason of their greater elasticity, have a great advantage over nails for building in the hurricane belt.

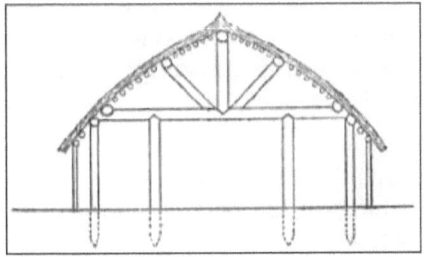

The Niuéan style of house-building so closely resembles the Tongan that it is difficult to believe that the one has not been copied from the other. Alofi Church, a fine native building with concrete walls, is almost as imposing as the best of King George's churches. Into one of the wall-plates the builder has worked a bifurcated tree-trunk, skilfully trimming it so that each prong shall bear an equal share of the weight of the beam.

When we reached the path to the Tongan cave at the southern end of the village our train had swelled to half a dozen voluble young men and a shy little girl. The cave was a rent in the limestone rock overgrown with creeping vines. A steep slope led down into an irregular gallery about twenty feet wide on the floor and narrowing to barely six feet at the narrowest part of the roof. The floor was very uneven, but in the lowest part, where there was a pool much encumbered with boulders, the cave must have been from thirty to forty feet high. Near the walls there was some depth of vegetable mould washed down from above, and I noticed that buckets were placed at intervals to catch the drip from the stalactites. This water, heavily charged with lime, was the drinking water of the village.

One of the men related the tradition of the cave, Mr. Lawes interpreting. In the days of the ancestors of old time a fleet of war-canoes was seen approaching from the west, and the warriors of Alofi made hasty preparations to receive what they knew to be an invading army. The women and children were sent into the thicket behind the rift, across which slender boughs were thrown, covered with soft earth to conceal the pitfall below. In the cave a chosen band of warriors was posted, armed with clubs. A war party of Tongans, leaping from the canoes, rushed up into the village, and was drawn towards the treacherous bridge by the retreating Niuéans, who knew where it was safe to cross. Dashing hot-foot in pursuit, the Tongans crashed through the false covering into the cave beneath, where they lay with broken limbs at the mercy of a clubbing party which knew no mercy. Only a remnant of stragglers stopped short of the pitfall and regained the canoes. And if we doubted the truth of the tradition, here in the soft earth were bones—the bones of those invaders of old time; and our escort fell to upon the proof, using their naked hands for spades. Bones there were certainly, but since the Niuéans laid the bones of their own dead in caves until the missionaries introduced the fashion of European burial, he would be a bold man who would swear to their nationality.

Now, mark how history is written by the savage as well as by the civilised man. I had heard a Tongan tradition of the invasion of Niué, and when I returned to Tonga I induced old Lavinia, the highest chief lady in the group and the guardian of ancient lore, to relate it again.

Fifteen generations ago, that is to say about 1535, Takalaua, King of Tonga, was assassinated by two old men, Tamajia and Malofafa, who had taken upon themselves the duty of avenging the miseries of their country. Pursued by his eldest son, Kau-ulu-fonua, they put to sea, and fled from island to island until they came to Futuna, where, because it was the end of the world and they could flee no further, they made a stand, and, being captured, were forced by their conqueror to chew his kava with their toothless and bleeding gums. From this horrible draught, swallowed in the ecstasy of triumph, Kau-ulu- fonua earned his surname of Fekai (the Cannibal). Among the islands visited by Kau-ulu-fonua in his pursuit of his father's murderers was Niué, and here, as the Tongan tradition has it, he landed on a small outlying islet, divided from the main island by a narrow chasm, into which the Niuéans, not knowing the stuff of which Tongan warriors are made, confidently expected that they would fall, if they essayed to cross. In this false security the defenders of the island assembled on the landward side of the chasm, and strove to terrify the invaders into retreating to their ships. But they fell into their own trap, for the Tongans, taking the chasm at a leap, slew hundreds of them, and cast the bodies of the slain into the depths below. And just as there are English and German and Belgian, if not French, historians to claim the victory at Waterloo, so Tongans and Niuéans tell the story each in their own fashion, and are happy.

That the tradition is history cannot be doubted. The Tongans relate that in the assault upon the walled fortress of Futuna, in which the murderers had taken refuge, a man, marvelling at the prowess of Kau-ulu-fonua, cried, "Thou art not brave of thyself, but by favour of the gods!" and that the chief retorted, "Then let the gods defend my back, and leave my front to me"; that as he was rushing through a breach in the wall he was wounded in the back, and cried, "The gods are fools!" An old man of Futuna, whom I asked whether there were any traditions of a foreign invasion, replied that the Tongans once assaulted his island, led by a chief who cried, "The gods are fools!" and that as a punishment for his impiety so many of his warriors were slain that stacks were made of the dead bodies. It is scarcely possible that by mere coincidence such an incident could be common to the history of two peoples who have had no intercourse for generations.

CHAPTER II

AFFAIRS OF STATE

MR. LAWES' fears were relieved by the messenger who had carried my invitation to the king at Tuapa. The old gentleman, far from being offended at our choice of Alofi for the meeting, had beamed upon him with his left eye (the right is missing, and it was all he had to beam with), and was already half-way to the royal lodging in Alofi. The other messengers, returning from the more distant villages at intervals during the evening, brought back news no less favourable. Early in the morning persons sent out to reconnoitre reported that men were erecting awnings on the green before the school-house, that the headmen of villages had all arrived, and that His Majesty was being helped into his uniform. Ten was the hour, and on the stroke of the hour Captain Ravenhill landed with the portrait of the Queen, sent from Windsor as a present to the king. The sun was very hot: English uniforms are not built for a thermometer above eighty in the shade, and there was therefore some excuse for our feelings when we walked on to the green and found three men trying to fasten a mat to four stakes planted anyhow in the grass. Half a dozen children were amusing themselves with a running commentary upon how not to rig an awning, and that was all.

The hour that we spent in the school-house was the sultriest of my experience, but it was cool and comfortable beside the language that might have clothed our thoughts had Mr. Lawes not been present. That we were impotent made it no better. There were no means of knowing whether the king's unpunctuality was an intentional slight or merely the innate inability of a native to keep an appointment, and there was no certainty that he would choose to come at all. But although, as the green began to fill with a gay-coloured, chattering crowd, I was at one moment almost resolved to get to business without His Majesty, I was restrained by the mortification of poor Mr. Lawes, who felt that he had been charged with the arrangements, and whose hope that his flock would do nothing to disgrace themselves was suffering so cruel a check. The messengers who trod heels in the road leading to the royal quarters brought back conflicting rumours. One said that the king was arraying himself in the new rifle-green uniform imported for him by a storekeeper; another that he was taking off his royal trousers at the behest of a Samoan teacher, who asserted that trousers were no trappings for an interview with the Queen's Commissioner; another that he had sent for a trusted councillor to decide whether, if he wore a Samoan petticoat, he might retain his military helmet with the cock-feather plume to which he clave. What Mr. Lawes did not know about the people was not worth knowing, and yet, so long have form and ceremonial been abandoned by the Niuéans, that he was still inclined to think that the king would stroll on to the green as if he was taking the air, despite these reports of elaborate preparations.

The awnings were rigged at last—one for us, floored with planks, at the door of the school-house, and the other facing it, with a couple of wooden chairs for Their Majesties, and benches for the retinue. A crowd of several hundred people—women and children for the most part—had assembled when a man ran in to say that the royal procession was coming up the road. There was but just time to post Amherst Webber with his camera when the procession burst from behind the angle of the Mission fence.

It was worth waiting for. I heard Mr. Lawes murmur, "Well, I never thought they would do this!" The procession was headed by a dozen men in slop clothes and villainous, billycock hats set at a rakish angle. They all carried spears and paddle-shaped clubs in either hand, and a similar rabble brought up the rear. In the middle of this grotesque bodyguard walked the king and queen, both in petticoats, as befits the sex to which they belonged, for if the queen was a young woman, the king was assuredly an old one. To their united ages of ninety-four His Majesty contributed seventy-six, but what he lacked in youthful elasticity he made up in condescension, for she had been but a beggar-maid—or what corresponds therewith in Niué, where beggary is unknown—when he had played Cophetua to her a few months before our visit. She wore a wreath of roses, he the soldier's helmet with the cock's plume, which was all that the officious Samoan teacher would leave him of his military uniform, and from which he refused to be divided, although it assorted ill with his petticoat. To tell the brutal truth, His Majesty was unsexed by the garments that had been chosen for him, and his appearance justified the remark of a friend who, holding the photographs of Their Majesties in his hand and confusing them, exclaimed, "Why, the queen's got a beard!" With the king was an angular old man in a strange, ill-fitting uniform and a tall hat of ancient date, carefully brushed the wrong way to show its wealth of nap; his uniform was bespattered with yellow anchors and other nautical devices, and he carried a spear in either hand. Though we could not discover that he had any connection with the court, he certainly imparted to the royal procession an air of dignity that it sadly needed.

THE ROYAL PROCESSION

The King dons a helmet and petticoats for the occasion

As soon as the royal party had taken their seats under the awning that faced ours the retinue fell upon the crowd with loud shouts, brandishing their paddle-shaped clubs, making thereby a louder disturbance than that which they were sent to quell; but the sight of Mr. Lawes standing forth to interpret produced what passes for silence in Niué. I gave my speech to Mr. Lawes sentence by sentence, using my old experience as an interpreter of South Sea languages to cast them in the form and length that are best suited to the translator. But, had I disguised my remarks in the language of the accomplished gentlemen who provide the copy for the halfpenny press, Mr. Lawes would have triumphed over all difficulties. Mindful of his gentle tones in conversation, I had suggested a doubt whether his voice would carry easily over the wide interval between the awnings, and had evoked from Mrs. Lawes an assurance that his voice would carry twice the distance. In truth its power and resonance were astonishing, and for once in my life I found it a positive pleasure to talk to a native through an interpreter. The similarity of Niuéan and Tongan was so close that I was able to appreciate the clever way in which he turned his sentences so as to convey the exact meaning without a superfluous word. After the usual compliments I explained that the Queen had answered the petition of the late king by taking Niué under her protection; that the people need never fear seizure of their country by one of the great Powers; that their young men working on plantations in other countries would henceforth be able to claim the protection of the British Consul; and that, as a token of her solicitude for their welfare, the Queen had sent them a portrait of herself to be the property of the Niuéan people. The picture, an engraving of Her Majesty in the robes of her Jubilee in 1887, was carried over to the king's awning. Then I improved the occasion by giving them the results of a little calculation I had made. Their island, denuded of its young men, had, in its record harvest, produced but seven hundred tons of copra, valued at six thousand pounds; if the young men who went abroad to earn twenty-four pounds a year were to stay at home and plant cocoanuts, they would soon be able to earn four times that amount from their own lands, money would flow into the island, the women who had neither husbands nor children would be bringing up families, and the chiefs, who now encouraged their young men to go abroad for the sake of the beggarly commission paid to them by the recruiting agent, would be richer than they had ever dreamed.

On the previous afternoon a travelled Niuéan had asked me anxiously whether the hoisting of the flag entailed *tukuhau*, the Tongan word for taxes, an institution unknown in Niué save by report, and justly dreaded on account of the stories brought back by those who had been in Tonga, where labourers are made to pay £1 16s. to the Government out of their wages. When I reassured him, the good news was passed down the line of our followers, who received it with enthusiasm. A repetition of this assurance as regards the immediate future made the most appropriate peroration to my speech.

The king, who had till now sat like a bronze image, so deeply sunk in his voluminous draperies that little could be seen of him but his helmet, now shook himself, and returned thanks in a formal speech, from which his real feelings could not be gathered; and I, warned by Mr. Lawes that if I once allowed the pent-up flood of oratory to find an open sluice, the river of talk would flow far into the night, went over to shake hands with him and to invite him to come into the school-house and sign the treaty. In Samoa, in Tonga, or in Fiji, this portion of the proceedings would have been invested with some solemnity; in Niué it was a children's game. The treaty was laid upon the schoolmaster's standing desk, and three separate messengers were despatched to bring ink, pens, and blotting-paper. The king sat apart in a Windsor chair; the headmen, under the guise of electing three of their number to witness the king's signature, were boiling over with jealousy; a troop of children were playing noisily at the far end of the school-house, and near us a woman was sitting on the floor, placidly suckling her baby. Outside three of the club- bearers were haranguing the crowd, which, having much to say on its own account, did not listen to them. We had almost to shout to make ourselves heard, until some new attraction took the fancy of the idlers, the earth shook to the thud of running feet, and the orators were left to harangue to the babies who were too tiny to run.

Now a difficulty arose. On the most liberal allotment of space—and Niuéan calligraphy demanded full measure—there was room in the treaty for but three signatures besides the king's. Eleven villages, and space for only three! It meant that three headmen would be represented to Queen Victoria as pre-eminent above their fellows. Mr. Lawes had been listening to the discussion, and he hastened to assure me that unless space could be found for four at least there would be trouble, for it meant that the headman of Alofi would be left out. The other seven mattered but little, for they were either amiable nonentities themselves, or their villages were too insignificant to matter. Room had to be made for Alofi, but his fingers were so tremulous with indignation at the suggested insult that they could scarcely hold the pen.

When the treaty was signed, I invited the chiefs to ask me questions, suggesting at Mr. Lawes' instance that the king should be their spokesman. His Majesty, fixing his single eye upon me, began in a plaintive voice to recite the wise acts of his reign. He desired me to take note that he had enacted two laws which would never be abrogated: the one forbidding the sale of land to Europeans, and the other prohibiting the sale of intoxicating liquor to his people. I hastened to assure him that these wise enactments (in which I suspected the guiding hand of Mr. Lawes) had my full approval, provided that no difficulties were thrown in the way of leasing land to Europeans for trading purposes. This, the king assured me, was never the case; they liked Europeans, and if their young men stole things from them, the community made restitution and punished the culprits. What they wanted was advice, and if the Queen sent an adviser to live among them, it would be well. He agreed with me that it was ill to denude the island of its young men, and I might count upon him to discourage the practice.[2] Finally he commended Niué-Fekai to the keeping of God, who had showed His favour to her this day in uniting her to England—the "greatest nation in the world."

A messenger, who now arrived from the landing-place, explained the defection of the crowd outside. A party had landed from the *Porpoise* to erect the flagstaff that we had brought from Sydney. As soon as the people understood their purpose, the crowbars and shovels were snatched from the hands of the blue-jackets, and the natives themselves, with shouts of laughter, fell to with a will upon the grave of their independence. The blue-jackets, nothing loath to exercise their unaccustomed rôle as foremen of works, were laughingly directing operations, when some officious elders, scandalised by what they considered to be a breach of manners, fell upon the volunteers with their paddle-clubs and drove them off, though not before the happiest relations had been established between the natives and their visitors.

CHAPTER III

THE KING OF ALL NIUÉ

FOR a few hours His Majesty could lay aside the cares of state, and I was able to make his acquaintance. He faced the camera without a trace of embarrassment, though he had probably never seen one before, and he consented, at my entreaty, to be photographed without his helmet. He is a withered, grey-bearded, querulous old man, and he looks the age assigned to him—seventy-six; but, despite the ravages of age and the blemish of a missing eye, there is an air of decision and obstinacy about him which does not belie his character. For it is by sheer tenacity of purpose that Tongia has attained his present giddy eminence.

The institutions of Niué have always been republican. In heathen times the king was theoretically an officer elected by the people; in practice he was a figure-head set up by the war-party (*toa*) who happened to have the upper hand for the moment. And since, in the see-saw of intertribal warfare, Fortune sometimes frowned upon his supporters, and the hopes of the opposition were always centred in the murder of the king, from the day of his election he went in peril of his life. In fact, a violent death was so often the portion of the titular ruler of the island that it became as difficult to find a candidate for royal honours as it was to discover a person to serve heir to a *damnosa hereditas* in Rome before Justinian. About the middle of the last century the supply failed altogether: for eighty years there was no king at all, and the island seems to have got on very well without one. But with the arrival of the missionaries and the cessation of war the office was discovered to have some attractions, and Tuitonga, a chief of Alofi, leaned his back against the stone[3]
—the time-honoured symbol of the assumption of supreme power. His successor, Fataäiki, also of Alofi, was described by Commodore Goodenough as the most remarkable chief he had seen in the Pacific, and, at his death in 1897, no one was found worthy to succeed him. His son, the young man who had acted as our pilot, was addicted to strong waters, and even if he had been otherwise eligible, he had put himself out of court by refusing to vacate the house built by the people as an official residence, but, owing to an oversight, erected on Fataäiki's private land. There was an interregnum for two years, and only one man in the island thought that there need ever again be a king of Niué-Fekai.[4] That man was Tongia.

Tongia was headman of Tuapa, and if he had attained no greater eminence until he was past seventy, it was owing to no foolish modesty on his part. You may, it seems, choose your own surname in Niué, and the name he chose in early life was Folofonua, which is "Horse"—the most terrible of all the beasts known to the men of that day. When horses lost their terrors and became vulgar, he took a name more awe-inspiring still—Puleteaki, which is "Great Ruler"; but, lest men should forget his importance for lack of reminder, he changed that for Tongia, the highest title he knew. A full year he waited for someone to suggest an election to the throne, and then, at one of the monthly councils, he took the matter in hand himself. As no one seemed to covet the dignity, how would it do, he asked, to elect *him*? When they had recovered from their astonishment, his colleagues adduced reasons enough why it would not do: to begin with, they had done very well without a king, and (if he would have the brutal truth) should they ever find themselves in need of one, there were ten other good men and true from whom to choose. They, in fact, were adamant, but Tongia knew that drops of water will wear even adamant away. He had experienced seventy years of opposition, and he had always had his way in the end. He dangled the empty crowning-stone before them at Fono after Fono, until in very weariness they let him have his will of them. It made little difference to them then, for in Niué there is no civil list. The king lives like any other landowner, on the produce of his own plantation, and the rent which his poor relations pay him in kind. Occasionally, when these fail him, he suggests how becoming it would be in his people if they were to bring him an offering of food, or even money, and they, mindful of the manner in which their liege lord attained his present dignity, murmur, "Anything for a quiet life," and hasten to stop his mouth.

Whether he is begging or merely asserting his importance, there is an air of conscious rectitude about Tongia that is impressive. Like most men who have done great things in the world, he has no sense of humour; I do not think he has ever been known to smile. He has gone through life in a deadly earnest, beside which the purpose in other men was but the purpose of butterflies. He had been but a few days king when he heard of the Queen's Jubilee of 1897. "Has the Queen of England been told of me?" he asked Mr. Head. "What? Has no one thought of telling her that I am king of all Niué—of Niué-Fekai?" Yet he must not be called vain, if the old definition be just which sets forth that "the conceited man is he who thinks well of himself and thinks that others do so too; the vain man is he who thinks well of himself and *wishes* that others thought so too; but the proud man is he who thinks well of himself and does not care a jot whether others think well of him or not." Upon this exegesis Tongia is a proud man. Knowing that he was versed in ancient lore, I asked him some questions about the Niué custom in time of war. "Tell him," he said to Mr. Lawes, "that the greatest warrior of old time was my father. There has been none like him in the world before or since." I tried my question in three several forms, but His Majesty, knowing better than I what I wanted to know, entertained me with anecdotes of his dashing father until I dropped my point.

KING TONGIA

In order to give éclat to the ceremony of hoisting the flag, which is in itself a somewhat brief and barren entertainment, I had asked Captain Ravenhill to invite the volunteer drum and fife band belonging to the ship to take part in it. He objected that the band had not played together for many months, but as the Niuéans had never heard a band of any kind, and were not likely to be a critical audience, we decided to send the invitation. Half an hour later the island was startled by the spirited performance of the "British Grenadiers." It brought the whole population to the flagstaff at a run, and I doubt whether musicians ever played to so attentive an audience since Joshua's trumpets played their symphony before the walls of Jericho. We needed no crier to remind the people of the historic hour; when the guard of honour landed not even a dog was missing. The sky had clouded, and a gentle rain was falling as the guard formed up, but ere I had done reading the proclamation, the sun came out to see another gap in its course filled by the flag on which it never sets. As the signalman slowly ran up the Jack, the band played the National Anthem, and a royal salute thundered from the guns of the ship lying at anchor below us. To stand at the salute in a hot sun until the whole twenty-one guns have been fired is a tedious ordeal, and I could not help my eyes ranging right and left of me to the faces of the crowd. It was a strange scene. Here were some thousands of natives, clad for the most part in clothes made by the slop-tailors of Europe, gazing in open-mouthed wonder at a handful of officers in gold-laced uniform performing a ceremony intended in some way to change the tenour of their lives. And behind lay the island, unchanged and unchangeable through the centuries. Overhead were the trees that had looked down upon the assault upon Cook by the native grandsires of these orderly Christians, who set upon him "with the fury of wild boars," brandishing paddle-clubs, and throwing these same lances that arm the king's bodyguard. The foreigner has been too strong for them, but the island will be too strong for the foreigner. The foreigner has landed and brought with him the disease they feared so much, but let him hoist flags and fire guns once a week until the Last Trump, he will never conquer the stern fact that the island lies remote from the great highways of the ocean, and turns a frowning cliff, against which the great rollers shatter themselves unavailingly, upon those who would beguile her into commerce.

HOISTING THE UNION JACK OVER SAVAGE ISLAND

April 21st, 1900

With the smoke of the last gun still floating in the air, I turned to congratulate the king upon being now under the protection of Her Majesty. He shook hands with me and thanked me in a bewildered way. And looking round upon

29

these hundreds of "British Protected Persons," who had changed their international status so suddenly, I could not help wondering what they (or, indeed, anybody else) thought had been effected by the change.

And here let me say a word about Protectorates. The word was invented by the lawyers a few years ago when the scramble for the world began, and there are those who think that if the man who first conceived the idea had been led out quietly to a lethal chamber, the world would have been saved a great deal of worry and vexation. In the old days when a nation wanted a land it took it, dishonestly, it may be, but at least openly, and tried to govern it after such fashion as lay within its power. But when the scramble began, the European Powers had to invent a polite way of saying to one another, "We have taken this country, not because we mean to use it, but because we do not mean you to have it! We take it under 'our protection.'" Under the old system nations recognised some responsibility towards the land they seized; they were at least responsible for its good government; under the new they recognise none except the duty of crying "Hands off!" to the others, until action is forced upon them by internal disorder. Now mark the hair-splitting that ensues. No man can serve two masters. The men of Niué owe allegiance to their own sovereign; they cannot also owe it to the Queen; and a man who owes no allegiance to the Queen cannot be a British subject. And yet when you guarantee him protection at home, it would be unreasonable to refuse him protection while sojourning abroad. If not a British subject, yet something British he must be. The lawyers had to invent another term, and they called him a "British Protected Person." When a black man is a British subject it is bad enough. A Fijian residing in Tonga has a child by a Tongan woman. If he was legally married to her the child is British, and must be tried by a British court; if they were not legally married it is Tongan, and is under the jurisdiction of Tongan magistrates. And the wretched consul has to test the legality of the native marriage. If it was a heathen marriage the case is worse, for the courts have never settled whether heathen marriages, performed after the custom of the country, are marriages at all in the eye of the law of England. But when a "British Protected Person" has a child, we are treading upon thin ice indeed, and I presume that every consul follows the dictates of such conscience as he may have left to him. One need not go further than Siam to see how the system may be abused. You have only to rake in half the population as Protected Persons to establish a very fair claim to the Protectorate of the soil on which they live, and this is precisely what the French Consul, by inscribing all disaffected Siamese as French citizens, is doing.

The invention of the Protectorate is, of course, very useful in certain cases. Many of the Pacific Islands are the natural heritage of the future Australian people, and it would have been most unfair to them to allow alien nations to seize upon points of vantage about their very gates. It would have been equally unfair to the English taxpayer and to the natives of the islands to assume the government of countries that were content to be under the authority of their own chiefs. If the idea of the Protectorate had entered the heads of politicians sixty years ago, the French would not now own Tahiti and New Caledonia, nor the Germans the Marshalls, the Northern Solomons, and Northern New Guinea.

There are Protectorates and Protectorates. In some you may have a resident adviser who virtually rules the country; in others a resident who is there to give advice when it is asked for; in others no resident at all. To the first class belong Zanzibar and the protected states of India; to the second, Tonga and Somaliland; and to the third, Niué; but in every class the establishment of a Protectorate is probably the prologue to annexation more or less delayed. Why then was the flag hoisted? There is, in fact, no reason why the flag should be hoisted in a Protectorate, for the mere hoisting of a piece of bunting is not in itself an act of appropriation recognised by international lawyers. At one time or another the British flag has been hoisted in many parts of the world that now belong to other nations. The legally recognised act is the reading of a proclamation, and of this the flag is a mere symbol that adds nothing to the legality when it is there, nor takes away from it when it is absent. As a general rule the flag is not hoisted in countries that have a flag of their own. It has never been hoisted in Zanzibar nor in the protected states of India. On the other hand, a people like the Niuéans, who have no flag, and know that other countries have one, would never consider the Protectorate effective unless they were granted the outward symbol of their allegiance. As the matter had been left to my discretion, I had no hesitation in giving them what they wanted. Fortunately none of the complications attending a Protectorate had time to arise in Niué, for six months later the island was formally annexed to the Colony of New Zealand.

The king had a request to make. He had never been on board a man-of-war. Would the captain invite him to pay the ship a visit that very afternoon? The eleven headmen also had requests to make: they too would like to be of the party. As each of the eleven would have brought two friends, and each friend two cousins, Captain Ravenhill was advised by Mr. Lawes to make stern discrimination. The captain's boat would be sent for the king, the queen, and the king's son. No one else, on pain of the captain's severe displeasure, was to take passage in her, but the eleven would be welcomed provided that they came alone and found their way off in their own canoes. Their Majesties were punctual, and the boat was got away with Mr. Head's son, a well-educated half-caste, as interpreter, and not more than two interlopers. All went well until she neared the ship, and then the queen, after a whispered consultation with her consort, began to take off her boots. This operation being still in progress long after the boat was alongside the gangway, faces began to peer curiously over the side, but the blue-jacket stationed at the foot of the ladder preserved an admirable composure, and, when Her Majesty had paddled up the steps in her stockings, he gravely followed the procession, carrying the royal boots as if they were insignia of office, to the suppressed merriment of his fellows, who were drawn up to receive the royal party. After the usual entertainment in the captain's cabin the king was shown over the ship. Neither the big six-inch guns, nor the neat little three-pounders that are fired from the shoulder like a shot-gun, seemed to impress him, and it was not until he was shown into the chart-room that he began to show enthusiasm. Deceived by the brass chimney of the heating stove, he declared it to be the finest kitchen he had ever seen. It was in vain for the interpreter to explain the real uses of the room. It was the kitchen—anyone could see that for himself—and if the captain chose, for reasons of his own, to lie about its real uses, he, Tongia, was too old in the craft of this world to be taken in. When I questioned him afterwards about his visit, he said without hesitation that the part of the ship that he had most admired was the kitchen, and he clung to the idea with the same tenacity that had won him the throne. When the interpreter had hinted to him that it was time to take leave, the king, producing a dollar from his waistband, signified his intention of tipping the captain for the pleasant entertainment he had provided, and the interpreter had the greatest difficulty in persuading him that such an act would be contrary to the decencies of European custom. A dollar was a very precious possession in the king's eyes, and it puzzled him, after many years' experience of the breed, that any white man should refuse to pocket money when it was offered him. The king was half-way down the ladder when he turned back, and the smile faded from the countenance of the captain, who thought that he was in for a second visit; but it appeared that Tongia had suddenly remembered the foreign custom of giving precedence to ladies, and he gallantly motioned to the queen to precede him, and handed her boots down after her. At that moment he caught sight of the red ensign flying at the fore, and asked the captain to give him one like it. Pointing with some contempt to the Jack floating proudly from the flagstaff on shore, he said that the red ensign was the flag for him, the other being too dingy for his taste. With great tact Captain Ravenhill explained that the red ensign was the badge of merchant ships and second-class potentates, and that, on seeing the Jack, visitors would at once recognise the importance of Niué-Fekai, and would conduct themselves with a proper spirit of respect.

THE QUEEN OF NIUÉ

CHAPTER IV

A TRIP THROUGH THE ISLAND

O N a sunny afternoon we took horse and rode to Tuapa, the royal village. The road was a grassy path vaulted with palm fronds and walled with dense undergrowth. Though it followed the trend of the coast, and was never more than a few hundred yards from the edge of the cliff, the foliage was so dense that we seldom caught sight of the sea below us. I imagined in my innocence that we should cover the seven miles at a hand gallop, the ordinary pace of horses in Tonga, but in less than a hundred yards I discovered the difference between a Niuéan and a Tongan road. The couch grass that looked so soft and springy was as specious as the thin earth which a gamekeeper sprinkles over the teeth of his gin. Taking root in little pockets of earth, it sent out a tangle of runners over the jagged projections of coral, which it just served to hide, so that the poor unshod horses could not avoid them. My beast knew his business, which was to walk daintily, like a cat on hot bricks. He had his frogs to mind, and when I forced him into a canter he obliged me for half a dozen paces, just to show me what pain I was giving him. After that we let our horses choose the pace they preferred, which was something under three miles an hour. We passed hundreds of natives dispersing from the meeting at Alofi, among them four men who were carrying the Queen's picture, shoulder high, on a sort of bier. Men and women alike, they all had a smile for us, and most of them a word of greeting to Mr. Flood, who had not only lent us the horses, but was acting as our guide. We passed through three villages of white cottages, not arranged on any plan, as in Alofi, but straggling among the trees in a most picturesque fashion. On the seaward side the way was dotted with graves, sometimes in clusters, oftener in twos and threes. They varied from an oblong cairn of stones, with a white headstone of concrete, to a neat domed tomb, carefully trowelled off, so as to leave the name of the deceased in bas-relief characters of irregular shape, six inches in length. The fashion of burying the dead was introduced by the missionaries, for in former times (and unlike the Tongans, who always buried their dead in graves, even where caves abounded) the Niuéans used occasionally to lay their dead in canoes and let them drift out to sea; but more generally they laid the body on a platform of stones in the bush, under a coverlet of bark cloth (*hiapo*) until nothing was left but the bones, which they gathered up and deposited in a cave. During the lying-in-state a kind of wake was held on the ninth day, and repeated at intervals until the hundredth, and during the earlier stages the body was frequently washed. In the little island of

Nayau, in Fiji, I once visited one of these natural catacombs. The steep and rocky path by which it was approached was polished by the feet of the generations of mourners that had passed over it. In the cave itself the dead were laid in a neat row. In the more recent cases the skeletons were entire, and fragments of the mats that had swathed the bodies still lay about them; but further in the bones had crumbled, bats' droppings had mingled with the dust, and the teeth and a few fragments of the jaws were all that was left.

The attention now paid to graves in Niué is due less to the influence of the Mission than to the superstition of the people. The Mission has never been able to cure them of their belief in ghosts. When a man is sick to death his friends bring him food (which he is long past eating) and say, "Grant our request; if go you must, go altogether." But his dying promise is not enough. As soon as the breath is out of him they lay a fragment of white bark cloth beside the body, and sit watching for an insect to crawl on to it. The insect is the dead man's *mou'i*, the soul (literally, "life"), and it is carefully wrapped up and buried with the body. The grave having been dug and the body, washed, oiled, and wrapped in bark cloth, laid in it, heavy stones are piled upon it to keep the *aitu* down. The dome of concrete, plastered without a crack, is generally enough to baffle the most restless ghost, but there have been cases when it has defied even this precaution. About the year 1898 a woman, who had thus buried her daughter, fell ill of a lingering malady, which could only have been caused by the malevolence of the dead girl's ghost. With infinite difficulty she collected a load of firewood, which she stacked over the grave and ignited, reducing the limestone rock to powder. From that day she steadily recovered, and in that village, at all events, superstition will die hard.

At a village near Alofi we left the road to examine the bathing-cave, which proved to be a rift in the limestone—a cavern whose roof had fallen in. Scrambling down its steep sides, we found the water about sixty feet below the surface. It was an oblong pool, about eighty feet long and twenty broad, green, brackish, and forbidding. Somewhere in its mantling depths there must have been communication with the sea, for the water rose and fell with the tide. It was difficult to understand how anyone, for the sake of some twenty per cent. less salt in the water, could prefer this stagnant pool, striking icy cold from the grim shadow of the rock, to the sunlit sea so near at hand. In the same village there was a natural well, which Mr. Lawes had commended to me as being the one place where really fresh drinking water was to be had. It was a mere crack in the rock by the side of the footpath, eight inches by twelve, and the gear for drawing water was a little canvas bucket with a sinnet string attached. By measuring the string we found its depth to be sixty-three feet. It was a hot day, and we fell eagerly upon the clear, cool water, but a mouthful was enough. A tumblerful of spring water with a teaspoonful of salt well stirred would have tasted fresh in comparison. I gently chaffed Mr. Lawes about his well afterwards, and he then admitted that it was an acquired taste, but that for his part he found the water of other countries a little insipid.

We found Tuapa almost deserted, for we had overtaken the greater part of its population on the road. It is as large as Alofi, but more irregular, and, if the truth be told, the palace of His Majesty is the meanest and ugliest building in it. I was constrained to drop my voice when I said so, for it seems that his palace is not the least of King Tongia's claims to fame, seeing that it shares with the dwelling of the late king the distinction of being the only native house in the island roofed with corrugated iron. If I had told him that there were many dogs in England lodged in houses of more pretentious size, he would (if I understand the old gentleman's character) not have put an end to his existence; on the contrary, he would have asked me for the ground plan of Buckingham Palace, and have worried his council until they had got to work upon an edifice a size larger.

A few miles beyond Tuapa the road breaks away from the sea so as to cut off the north end of the island. The bush is denser, the way more wild and lonely, and, night coming on, we were obliged to turn back to Tuapa to sleep. And yet, though none but the European traders own carts, the natives have made all these roads, with the exception of a bad bit between Alofi and Avatele, available for wheel traffic. The Pacific Islands Company is doing its best to persuade the people to buy and use carts, but a people who cheerfully carry to market on their backs a sack of copra weighing close upon a hundredweight for a distance of nine miles do not see any point in labour-saving contrivances.

Mr. Flood was good enough to show me the contents of his store. The products of civilisation that tempt natives are much the same throughout the Pacific. Axes and knives come first, of course; looking-glasses and umbrellas run them hard for second place; prints, and sewing-machines to make them up with, and (alas!) slop clothing have now become necessities. For luxuries there are pipes and plug tobacco and cheap scents and a hundred other things, but there are certain articles that you will not find in a native store. The Niuéans want no hats; they make them for themselves and for others, the export of straw hats to New Zealand having been a few years ago three thousand dozen. These hats are plaited very cleverly by the women from the leaves of the pandanus and a similar leaf imported from Anuia in the New Hebrides. The manufacturer got a shilling, and the middleman only tenpence, which sounds curious until you learn that the manufacturer was paid in trade, and then you understand where the middleman came in. Unfortunately the market was overstocked, and the export fell away to nothing, but this year it is reviving. You will find neither combs nor spades, for the native makes his own comb, and finds a digging-stick the more handy tool in his garden.

The traders make no fortunes in Niué. In normal years the whole export of the island is about three hundred and fifty tons of copra, a few hats, and eight tons of fungus, which finds its way to China to be food for mandarins. Arrowroot might be grown in any quantity if there were any demand for it. The export of fungus is now decreasing, owing to the fall in price. At the liberal valuation of £9 a ton for the copra, and allowing for the money brought back by the returned emigrants, the entire income of the island is under £3,500 a year, and upon this modest sum the natives have to satisfy their new wants, the Mission teachers and several independent traders have to live, and a fair margin of profit has to be found for the shareholders of two trading companies, after paying the salaries of their local employés. In 1899, however, the export of copra reached the unusual figure of seven hundred tons, and the island was passing rich.

The first trader to settle in the island was the late Mr. H. W. Patterson, who came from Samoa in 1866 as agent for Messrs. Godefroy and Son, of Hamburg. For some years this famous firm had almost a monopoly of the trade of the Pacific. In 1866, owing to the American civil war, kidney cotton fetched 20 cents a pound. The export from Niué increased year by year until 1880, when it fell to 7 cents. For a brief period it advanced to 10 cents, and then it fell so low that it is not worth growing. Mr. R. H. Head, who landed in January, 1867, began to trade as agent for the notorious Bully Hayes, pirate and blackbirder. He was the first to buy fungus, which reached its highest export about 1880. Copra, which was not manufactured until 1877, is now almost the only export.

At present the cocoanuts planted on Niué consist of a strip along the western coast that widens into patches on the sites of the villages. The trees were in rude health, and I do not doubt that every acre on the island would grow nuts with a trifling expenditure of labour in clearing and planting. The cocoanut palm must have been specially designed by Providence for South Sea Islanders, for after the first five years it takes care of itself, and will continue to bear nuts though its roots are choked by undergrowth. All that its owner has to do is to collect and split the fallen nuts, exposing their kernels to the sun, which shrivels the pulp until a shake will free it from the shell. A sack and a sturdy pair of shoulders will carry the dried kernel—now converted into copra—to the nearest store, where it is worth a shilling for every ten pounds. The traders are able to give this high retail price, because they pay in "trade," and not in money. Their profit is made out of the calico, etc., accepted by the native as the equivalent for the shilling. To even the laziest native an occasional short spurt of energy is pleasant, and his copra having provided him with a change of clothes, a tin of biscuits, and a gallon of lamp oil, he can lie on his back for the rest of the year. Copra, it must be remembered, has nothing to do with his daily subsistence, for which nature has provided in other ways. In the bread-fruit islands of the east he has only to bury the ripe fruit in a pit, and dig it up as it is wanted; in the west he has to plant his yams and taro, or set his wives to do it, as his fathers did before him. But the Niuéans are not lazy, and I could not help contrasting their neglect of so obvious a source of wealth with the greater energy in copra-making of the Tongan. It is here that the Mission comes in. But for the missionary collection it may be doubted whether some of the Polynesian races would plant cocoanuts at all, and I do not think that justice has been done to the value of the Wesleyan missionaries, who always run their missions on a good business basis, as fosterers of commerce. When the Tongan has bought his small luxuries and paid his taxes, the native ladies who are to have basins at the missionary collection (as Englishwomen hold stalls at a bazaar) begin to tout for constituents. The chain of emulation is most skilfully forged. Each basin-holder vies with her neighbour; each of her constituents vies with his fellows who shall attain the glory of making the largest contribution. The missionary has simply to set the delicately balanced machine in motion, and wait until it showers dollars into his lap. The basin-holders do the rest. "Paul has promised to give five dollars: you beat Paul last year!" and Peter sets forth next morning with his splitting-hatchet to split nuts enough to make six dollars. Out of this copra the trader sucks his profit. From the mercantile point of view this is to be put to the credit side of the account: with its other side I have dealt with elsewhere.[5]

The London Missionary Society appears to care more for the work of its churches and schools than for its balance-sheet, and to practise no method for swelling its collections. And as the Niuéans have as yet few wants, and are subject to no sudden calls for money, they leave tree-planting alone, and expend their energy in road-making, in house-building, and in working for white men in other islands. If they were to spend but one day a month in planting cocoanuts for the next five years, they might double their export of copra. But their needs are growing, and with instincts so keenly commercial they are unlikely long to leave the potential wealth of their island unexploited.

In view of the enormous tracts of land throughout the tropic zone that have lately been planted with cocoanuts, it is remarkable that copra has maintained its price. In Ceylon I saw hundreds of acres planted with trees in full bearing, where scarce a tree was to be seen twelve years ago. From both coasts of Africa and from the West Indies the export has been steadily increasing, and yet, though the world seems to be easily sated with every other kind of tropical product, of copra it never seems to have enough. Handicapped by a sea-carriage of twelve thousand miles, the South Sea Island copra has always commanded a local price of from £8 to £11 a ton, and now that a soap and candle factory has been established in Australia, it is more likely to rise than fall. Ten years ago most of the copra went direct to Europe on German sailing ships, which came out to Australia with a general cargo and loaded copra in the islands. In the long homeward voyage of from four to six months the rats and the little bronze copra-beetles tunnel through the cargo, destroying large quantities. On arrival at the oil mills it is crushed by rollers, and the refuse, after every drop of oil has been squeezed out of it, is pressed into oil-cake for fattening cattle. The oil is then resolved into glycerine and stearine, from which more than half the candles and soap used in the world are made. At first sight it would seem more economical to press the oil on the spot, and so save the freight upon the waste material; but the explanation is that oil must be shipped in tanks or in casks. Ships fitted with tanks would have to make the outward voyage empty, and casks, if shipped in "shooks," require expert coopers, and when soaked in oil become a prey to borers. It is possible that a new use may be found for copra as fuel for warships. Every ton of copra contains over one hundred gallons of oil besides other combustible matters, and it burns with a fierce heat. It is very easily stored and handled, and it is only one-third more bulky than coal, its disadvantage in this respect being more than compensated by its superior heating qualities and its freedom from ash. It is expensive, but as Welsh coal costs in distant stations such as China as much as £2 10s. a ton, it is only four times as dear, and in naval warfare, where quick steam is everything, the dearest fuel may often be the cheapest. It would be peculiarly suited to torpedo craft and destroyers, which are required to get up steam in a hurry, and to go short distances at enormous speed. I offer this suggestion to the Admiralty as a matter for experiment.

I have wandered far from the village of King Tongia, which was a curious peg on which to hang a digression on the markets of the world. Whatever the fates may have in store for Tuapa, it will never hum with the business of a trade centre. Our reluctance to anchor one of Her Majesty's ships at the seat of government was amply justified when I came to look at its so-called harbour. At this point the coast breaks away to the eastward, and even with the light easterly breeze that was blowing, there was a very respectable sea. With the wind inshore no ship could anchor and live. The cliff was so sheer that shoots had been built by which the bags of copra could be dropped to its base, and the little schooners that ship the copra have to watch the weather before they venture from the safer anchorage of Alofi. Mr. Head, the oldest trader on the island, told me that one morning several years ago his attention was attracted by seeing the natives running to the steep path that leads to the base of the cliff. Looking over, he saw them crowding about some object on the beach, and a mile to the northward a similar group was forming. Their gestures were so excited that he ran down the path to see what it was. Shouldering the natives aside, he was astonished to find a white girl of about eighteen, barefooted, half-laughing and half-crying at the perplexity of her case. For the natives were touching her to see whether she was real, and satisfied on that score, but baffled by her voluminous draperies, were proceeding in all innocence to more searching investigation, when Mr. Head fortunately intervened. While she was recovering from her hysterical laughter Mr. Head had time to remember that visitants from another world do not appear to mortals dressed in white flannel, albeit neither vessel nor boat was in sight. Yet her account of how she came to be one of the first white women to land on Niué was simple enough. She was not alone: farther up the beach he would find her father (Mr. Head remembered the second group of excited natives a mile away). He was the captain and owner of a little yacht a month out from Honolulu, and in the early morning they had landed to stretch their legs while the yacht lay off and on seeking anchorage. They thought the island uninhabited, and when her father wandered off and left her paddling in the warm sea, this crowd of wild savages had surrounded her, and she had made up her mind that she was to be eaten. While she was speaking, a trim little yacht, flying American colours, glided out from behind the point, towing her dinghy behind her.

Near Tuapa there is a cave which is dark at high noon. In its murkiest recess you may see a relic of the first civilised institution that took root in Niué—a set of stocks. The only punishments the Niuéans then knew were fines and the death penalty, and the stocks, which they appear to have seen in use on a whale ship, or more likely in Tahiti whither some of them were carried as slaves, were a notable discovery. The poor wretches thus imprisoned in the black hole of Tuapa were at least spared the dead cats and rotten eggs that were a recognised part of this punishment in England. When Hood visited Niué in 1862, a boy was lashed hand and foot to a bamboo for several days with just sufficient food to keep the life in him, as a punishment for tattooing himself after the Samoan fashion, to the scandal of the Niuéans who were never tattooed. Hood describes this as one of the ancient punishments.

Most fortunately for me the schooner *Isabel*, owned by Captain Ross, one of the most daring and successful navigators of these seas, arrived that day from New Zealand, bringing Mr. Head, who had been commended to me as the most suitable person to act as registrar to the Consul in Tonga, in whose province, as it was then intended, the new Protectorate was temporarily to be placed. I was a little bashful in approaching him with the offer, for twenty- three years ago Lord Stanmore, the High Commissioner, had offered him a similar post, and the letter of appointment was still to come. But finding that, despite his seventy years, he was still ready to accept the unpaid office, and that he was a *persona grata* to Europeans and natives alike, my hesitation vanished. I was particularly anxious to see him for another reason. He had lived more than forty years among the natives, and quite early in life he had married a Niué woman, with whom he still lived: consequently his knowledge of Niué customs was absolute and complete. To my great satisfaction a messenger arrived to announce that he had walked over to Tuapa in the dark, and that he invited me to spend the night with him. What he must have thought of me I dare not think, for blind to the fact that he had just landed from a rough voyage, and had tramped fourteen miles, I plied him with questions till past midnight. To me it was one of the most interesting evenings I have ever spent, but I blush now when I think of my inhumanity. To him and to Mr. Lawes I am indebted for all the ethnological information in this book. They agreed in every particular, and as Mr. Bell, a gentleman who had spent seven years in the island in the service of the Pacific Islands Company, to whom I showed my notes in Sydney, added his testimony, they may be accepted as accurate.

Mr. Head was the best specimen of an English trader that it has been my fortune to meet. He had had more than ten children by his native wife, and he was sufficiently educated to know the value of a good education. Nothing daunted by the gloomy forebodings of his friends, he determined to bring them up as European children. One after another, as they grew old enough, they were sent to school in New Zealand. All the sons that have stayed there are in good positions. Three have returned to Niué, where two help their father in his business, and a third has set up a store on his own account.

"'It's all very well with the boys, but what about the girls?' they used to say, but I think I have proved that half-caste girls are as good as any other if you give them a start," he said with quiet pride. One of his girls is married and prosperous in Auckland, another is a teacher in the public schools, and a third whom I met at Alofi would pass for a handsome, well-educated Italian. It was interesting to observe the manners of the boys towards their native mother when we met at breakfast. Mrs. Head wears the native dress and speaks English with hesitation, but she is an intelligent woman, and she plays the hostess at the head of her table admirably. She seemed a little shy of her English sons, but they spoke to her with courtesy and respect, and obliged her to take her fair share in the conversation. They have preserved the old fashion of addressing their father as "Sir." Thus has Mr. Head solved the problem that has baffled most fathers of half-caste children the world over.

CHAPTER V

SOME HISTORICAL RECORDS

I T would have astonished the first visitors to Niué not a little if they could have lived to see the island now. The first foreigner to land on the island after the Tongan invasion under Kau-ulu-fonua in the sixteenth century was Captain Cook, and his experience would have led no one to suppose that the natives would take kindly to strangers. They were, in fact, the only Polynesians who would have nothing to say to him. On Monday, June 20th, 1774, he landed on the north-west side of the island, at a spot probably not far from Tuapa, and, seeing no natives, rowed southward in his boat to a rift in the cliff, which, to judge from his description, must have been none other than Alofi. Here two canoes, hauled up upon the sand, tempted him to land, after his men had been posted on a rocky point to guard against surprise. He had not long to wait. Voices were heard in the thick undergrowth, and in a few minutes a band of men, naked save for a waistband, smeared from head to foot with black paint, and armed with throwing spears and slings, ran out into the open. His friendly gestures met with no response. They came at him "with the ferocity of wild boars and threw their darts." One of them struck Lieutenant Spearman on the arm with a stone from his sling, and another threw a spear at Cook at five yards that went near to ending the great navigator's career before ever he saw Hawaii. The spear missed his shoulder by a hair's-breadth, and the musket with which he tried to shoot the man missed fire, though when he afterwards fired it in the air, the powder exploded. The marines immediately opened fire, and at the report the natives took to their heels without suffering any loss. Cook wisely refrained from making further attempts to open relations with them, for the island was wooded to the edge of the cliff, and, the villages at that time being little fortresses in the interior, he saw no houses. Naming the place "Savage Island," a title which the natives now resent, he bore away to the north.

The first white man to land upon the island after Cook's visit did so under dramatic circumstances. It appears from the account of an aged native, who described the occurrence to Mr. W. G. Lawes as an eye-witness, that a whaler was lying off the island bartering with the natives, who were as wild and savage in appearance as Cook described them. As the ship got under weigh the master savagely threw one of his men overboard among the supposed cannibals, who took him ashore in their canoes. The natives were in great perplexity what should be done under such unprecedented circumstances. Many took their stand upon the ancient law. Salt water was in the stranger's

44

eyes—he must die! On the other hand, it was evident that the man had not landed of his own free will. The matter was settled by giving him a canoe victualled with bananas and cocoanuts and sending him out to sea. Returning to an unfrequented part of the coast under cover of night, he lay hid in a cave for several days, and succeeded in getting on board another whaler cruising in the neighbourhood.

In 1830 the pioneer missionary, John Williams, visited Niué in the *Messenger of Peace*,[6] on his way from Aitutaki to Samoa, where he intended to found a mission. Perceiving some natives on a sandy beach, which must have been the present landing-place at Avatele, he made signals of peace by waving a white flag, and, as soon as these were returned, he despatched a boat manned by natives only. They found the islanders drawn up in battle array, each having three or four spears, a sling, and a belt filled with large stones. They laid aside their arms as soon as they were satisfied that there were no Europeans in the boat, and presented the *utu*, or peace-offering, receiving small presents in return. This ceremony performed, they ventured out to the ship in their canoes, but Mr. Williams could prevail upon only one of them—the old man who endeavoured, with some success, to make the white men's flesh creep with the war dance—to come on board the ship. While he was retained as a hostage the boat party was permitted to land, but, night coming on, the hostage was landed, and the vessel stood out to sea. The old man had received with indifference an axe, a knife, and a looking-glass, but he broke into transports of joy when he was presented with a pearl shell.

On the following day Williams landed the two Aitutaki teachers and their wives, whom he intended to leave as pioneers of Christianity. They were "handled, smelt, and all but tasted," and, perceiving a vast multitude of natives gathering thoroughly equipped for war, they took alarm, and rowed off to the ship with one native, whom they persuaded to embark with them. This man wore the handle of an old clasp knife attached to his girdle, thus giving colour to the report that a few months earlier the natives had cut off a boat belonging to a passing vessel, and had murdered all the crew. The Aitutaki teachers, not unnaturally, objected to be left unprotected among these inhospitable people, and begged to be taken on to Samoa. To this Williams assented, not out of fear for their lives, which he thought would be in no danger, but because he thought it probable that they would be despoiled of everything they possessed.

He now set about inducing two natives to sail with him to the Society Islands, with the idea of restoring them to Niué after a course of instruction in the Mission school. With the greatest difficulty he persuaded two lads to embark, but no sooner did they see their island vanishing in the offing than they became frantic with grief, tearing their hair, "and howling in the most affecting manner." Nor would they eat, drink, or sleep for three days. They turned with disgust from meat and howled piteously, for, having never seen meat before, they took it for human flesh, and concluded that they had been taken on board as sea-stock for the voyage. On the third day, however, their fears were allayed by seeing a pig killed and cooked, and gradually they became reconciled to their new companions and pleased at the prospect of seeing new countries. They stayed some months with Williams in Samoa, and re-embarked with him in August, 1830, to return to their island. "Very favourable impressions had been made on one of them, but the other had resisted every effort to instruct him." Baffled by calms and light head winds, the ship ran out of provisions, and was compelled to bear away for Rarotonga without landing the boys, at which they showed much disappointment, until they were comforted by the assurance that by going first to Raiatea, they would be able to return home with more valuable presents. A few months later they were landed at Niué by Mr. Crook, one of the original missionaries who came out in the *Duff* in 1797, and Williams saw no more of them.

Perhaps it was as well. Dr. Turner, who visited Niué in 1848, says that shortly after the two lads' return influenza broke out, and they were accused of bringing the disease from Tahiti, which was not unlikely, seeing that Williams speaks more than once of its prevalence among the Mission families. One of the lads was killed, together with his father; the other contrived to escape in a whaler in company with a boy named Peniamina Nukai, who entered the Mission school in Samoa. In 1842 this boy returned to Niué in the Mission ship *Camden*, but so threatening was the attitude of his countrymen that he had to leave again by the same vessel. After another spell of four years in the school he returned to his island in October, 1846, in the *John Williams*. On his landing an armed crowd assembled to kill him. They wanted him to send his canoe, his chest, and all his property back to the ship, saying that the foreign wood would cause disease among them. He told them to examine the wood— it was the same that grew on their own island—and as for himself, how should he, a Niuéan like themselves, have more control over disease than they? Thereupon they broke up into two parties, the one for sparing his life, the other for giving him the shortest shrift. "Let us do it now," they said; "let us do it now while he is alone, and before the disease comes; presently others will join him, and it will be difficult." Night came on, but the people, fearing the infection, refused him shelter, and sent him to a deserted fortress, where he wandered about in the rain, until one man, moved either by compassion or scepticism, ventured to give him asylum for the night. Next day he began to display the treasures of his chest, purchasing many friends at the cost of his whole outfit.

The heathen priests, seeing their occupation in jeopardy, now set to work to compass his death by witchcraft, and perhaps much of the success of the Mission was due to the fact that he was too tough for their spells. Other villages began to wish that they had Mission teachers with the attendant blessings of hatchets and fish-hooks.

On August 29th, 1848, Dr. Turner, having obtained permission to send Samoan teachers to the island, sailed for Samoa with two more Niué boys to be trained in the Mission school. In October, 1849, a Samoan teacher named Paulo was landed at Avatele, and he was followed afterwards by four others, Amosa, Samuela, Sakaio, and Paula.

Captain Erskine touched at Niué in H.M.S. *Havannah* on July 6th, 1849, but did not land owing to the heavy swell from the westward. Numbers of the natives boarded the ship from their canoes, prepossessing Erskine favourably with their fearlessness and their honesty. One of them puzzled him by repeating the Samoan salutation of "Alofa!" and going through the pantomime of prayer, intending, doubtless, to inform him of the presence of Samoan teachers on the island.

Long before Dr. Turner's next visit in 1859 the whole population, with the exception of ten irreconcilables, was nominally Christian. The five Samoans had, indeed, changed the face of the country. The natives, formerly scattered about in little strongholds in the bush, were now congregating in settled villages round the school-houses; they had caught the garment-epidemic in its most aggravated form, and, as the missionary records complacently, they were all decently clothed from head to foot (we only, who have seen it, can realise the appalling nature of this reform); they had completed a six-foot road round the coast, which would "enable a missionary to take a horse all round the island, a distance of forty or fifty miles, perhaps"; they had abandoned war and infanticide; they no longer cut down the fruit-trees of the dead; they had even changed their manner of house-building. All this is an extraordinary result for five Samoans to have achieved unaided in half a dozen years.

The breaking down of the old system of exclusiveness was not an unmixed blessing to the islanders. Hitherto the whalers, knowing the reputation of the place, had given it a wide berth. As early as 1830 John Williams had found evidence in support of the story that they had cut off and murdered the boat's crew of a passing vessel, and in 1847 an American whaler lying off the island had not ventured to land to cut firewood until Peniamina showed the captain his paper of credentials as a Mission teacher. With the establishment of free intercourse the visits of ships became frequent. Whalers introduced a terrible disease; Bully Hayes, as will be presently related, found it a virgin field for "blackbirding."

DECENTLY CLOTHED FROM HEAD TO FOOT!"

The first European missionary who settled on the island was the Rev. G. Pratt, who was followed a few months later by the Rev. W. G. Lawes, now the head of the London Mission in New Guinea, the elder brother of our kind host. He came out direct from England with his wife in August, 1861, and found himself priest, prime minister, lawgiver, and physician all in one. He must have suffered terribly from the strain of isolation. Occasionally he obtained American papers from passing whalers—in one case a ship calling in 1862 supplied him with a Boston journal of 1834—but oftener he had the mortification of seeing ships pass in the offing without communicating with the shore. More than once English men-of-war actually had communication with the natives, but left again without knowing that there were white people on the island, or that there was a practicable landing-place.[7] Mr. Lawes' first intercourse with Englishmen took place in June, 1862, when H.M.S. *Fawn* (Captain Cator), the first steam vessel to visit Niué, put in, expecting to find the natives as Cook and Williams described them. Lieutenant Hood has left us an interesting account of this visit.[8] The natives were then in the first blush of their conversion. Less sophisticated than they are now, and as warm- hearted, they overwhelmed their visitors with the heartiness of their welcome. "Pleasant surprises," wrote Mr. Hood, "are amongst the most agreeable things in life. I don't remember ever being better pleased than with our reception at Savage Island." But the fever of foreign travel had already seized upon them. They importuned the captain to give them a passage in the ship; and it was then common, some days after whalers had left the coast, for two or three half-starved wretches to make their appearance from the hold. Force had generally to be used to drive the would-be emigrants into their canoes when a vessel was leaving, and it was reported that among the unhappy wretches labouring in slavery in the guano pits of the Chincha Islands were a few Savage Islanders.

The great enemy to the prosperity of the island is the labour trade. It began in 1865, when the Germans took a number of young men to work on their plantations in Samoa. In 1871 Messrs. Grice Sumner carried a number of men to Malden Island at a wage of ten dollars a month, half in trade and half in English money, with one month's wages paid in advance. This has been the regulation wage since that date, and it is not surprising that the island has been depopulated of its young men, for it is double the profit that can be made by tillage of the land in its present state, with the attractions of foreign travel thrown in. Nevertheless, if they only knew it, the Niuéans might become passing rich if they would stay at home and bestow their labour on the planting of cocoanuts.

In early life Mr. Head had been in the employment of Bully Hayes, the pirate. In the intervals of piracy Mr. Hayes had passed as a law-abiding trader, and it was only when he wearied of the slow returns accruing from the sale of calico that he turned to means of quicker profit. One day, in 1868, he put in unexpectedly at Alofi, and made himself so agreeable to the natives that sixty of them came off to his vessel to gloat over the wonder of a foreign ship. With that he slipped his cable and stood out to sea. The indignation of the islanders at this outrage knew no bounds. It was at its height when one morning, a week later, the joyful news spread that the ship was returning. Mr. Hayes landed alone, and met Mr. Head on the village green before all the natives. He was in high spirits, and had a ready answer to Mr. Head's reproaches. "I told the beggars that I was going to sail," he said, "but they wouldn't leave the ship. I couldn't stay here a month. What could I do?" The men, he told the natives, were all right. Finding that he had not provisions enough for so large a company, he had landed them at a nice little island to the northward, and had returned for food and water for the return voyage. If he had meant to kidnap them, would he have returned like this? The story was thin, but the natives were in no mood to test it. Provisions were shipped in quantities, and the crew of Aitutaki men landed and made friends with the people. That night word was brought to Mr. Head that these gentry had made plans to elope with a number of girls, whose heads they had turned with stories of foreign travel. He went at once to the chiefs, and a guard was despatched hotfoot to the beach, only to make out the schooner's lights in the offing. When they called the roll they found that more than thirty girls were missing. This was the last time Bully Hayes visited Niué. It was not till long afterwards that Mr. Head heard the sequel to the story. Re-embarking the men, whom he found half-starving, Hayes set sail for Tahiti, where he disposed of the whole of his cargo to the highest bidder, or, as he chose to put it, to the planter who paid the highest sum for their passage money. He had promised to bring them back in two years, but they heard no more of him. Many died in Tahiti; a few found their way to Samoa and Queensland; a remnant, in which was King Tongia's daughter, now a middle-aged woman, returned to Niué; the rest had scattered, who knows whither?

CHAPTER VI

THE ANCIENT FAITH

THE mythology of the Niuéans affords no key to the problem of their undoubtedly mixed origin, for it is purely Polynesian. As in New Zealand, Tonga, and many other Polynesian islands, Tangaloa and Mau'i were their principal deities—Tangaloa, the Creator, too august and remote to concern himself with human affairs; Mau'i, the sportive and mischievous, the Loki of Nibelung myth. Every village had its *deus loci*, who protected its crops in peace and its warriors in war, but, since there is no tradition of the earthly pilgrimages of these deities, there is no direct evidence to show that they were deified ancestors. One Niuéan story of the peopling of the earth is almost identical with the Maori myth as related by Sir George Grey. The Niuéan version is as follows. In the beginning of things Langi, the Heaven, lay locked in the embraces of his spouse, the Earth. Offspring were born to them, but because Langi would not leave their mother, they lay in perpetual night. So they took counsel together; and some were for killing both their parents; others were for forcing them apart, yet not so far but that their father should protect them from dangers above and their mother be close to nurse and feed them. The milder counsel prevailed. Uniting all their force, the men of those days pushed upwards and rent the pair in twain, nor desisted until the Heaven was set far above them and the light and air gushed in. Ever since that day the tears of Langi, thus severed from his bride, fall gently upon her, and in summer time his deep-toned lament terrifies the ears of men.

As another version of the myth has it, the wife of the first man complained that between the Heaven and the Earth there was not room for her to till the ground. The husband thrust his digging-stick upward, and pushed and pushed until something gave way, and the Heaven went up with a run.

In those days the ocean rolled unbroken over Niué. The god Mau'i, the same that drew Tonga to the surface with his entangled fish-hook, lying in a cave at the bottom of the sea, pushed up the floor of the ocean until it became a reef awash at low water. With another heave he sent it higher than the spray can reach, and birds settled upon it; seeds floated to it and germinated, and it became an island like to Tonga. Uprooting it with a last effort, he forced it to its present height, and, if you doubt the story, you have only to sail seaward and look back upon the cliff, where you will note galleries eaten into it by waves, marking its successive levels.

A third myth ascribes the creation of the island to Huanaki and Fao, two men who swam to Niué from Tonga. They found the island a mere reef awash at high water. They stamped upon it, and it rose, flinging the water from its sides. They stamped again, and up sprang the trees and grass. From a *ti* plant they made a man and woman, and from these sprang the race of men. At this time Mau'i lived just below the surface of the Earth. He prepared his food secretly, and his son, who had long been tantalised by the delicious smell of his father's food, lay in hiding to watch the process, and saw fire for the first time. When Mau'i was out of the way he stole a flaming brand and fled up one of the cave mouths into Niué where he set an *ovava* tree on fire. And thence it comes that the Niuéans produce fire from *ovava* wood by rubbing it with a splinter of the hard *kavika* tree.

A similar myth is current in the Union Group. An adventurous person named Talanga, having descended into the lower regions, found an old woman named Mafuike busied with a cooking fire. Compelling her by threats of death to part with her treasure, he enclosed the fire in a certain wood, which was consequently used by his descendants for making fire by friction.

There is a vast difference in the age of these myths. The Mau'i story, being common to other Polynesian races, belongs to the period before the Niuéans arrived in their island; the story of the two Tongans is probably a fragment of traditional history corrupted by Polynesian folklore. Huanaki and Fao were the ancestors of the race who drifted hither in a canoe with their women, perhaps through a westerly wind setting in while they were making the passage from Haapai to Vavau. That it was a chance drift, and not an organised immigration, is shown by the fact that there were no domestic animals in the island. Once cut off, the first immigrants seem to have lost all wish to seek their own land, which they might easily have done by building a canoe and running westward before the wind. They soon forgot how to make a sail. There is still current in Tonga a fragmentary tradition of a canoe belonging to the Tui Tonga having drifted to Niué in comparatively modern times. The Niuéans use the word "Tonga" to denote all foreign countries, and the best known of their kings bore the title of "Tui Tonga." Europeans were called *Koe tau mau'i*, after the Polynesian god, either from the wonders that they brought with them, or because they were supposed to come from the nether regions where Mau'i has his abode.

The oldest natives, when asked for an explanation of the name "Niué" shake their heads, and suggest that their ancestors, driven seaward from another island, and giving themselves up for lost, saw palms upon the island, and hailed them with the cry "Niu—é!" ("Palms ahoy!"); but that may be classed with a host of other native derivations of place-names, equally ingenious and equally improbable.

In the crowd at Alofi I noticed two distinct types of physiognomy, the one with wavy Polynesian hair and the large features of the Cook Islanders, and the other with lank, coarse hair and the Malayan features and rather oblique eyes of the Micronesians. These latter were comparatively rare—not more than ten per cent.

The exact origin of the people, now that the old men are fast dying off, can never be ascertained; but a clue may be found in the people of Avatele, the village at the south-west corner of the island. Even now they show traces of a distinct physical type, and in the last generation the short and thick-set frame, the large mouth and thick lips were very marked. They have, moreover, a higher reputation for bravery. They have several words not used in the other villages, and they speak with a peculiar sing-song, so that, as soon as an Avatele man opens his mouth, his speech betrays him. In olden times the whole island was against them, and they would certainly have been exterminated but for their fortress, which was *taue uka*—impregnable. It is situated at a place called Tepá, a little south of Avatele. The only entrance to it is a hole in the rock about three feet high and three feet six inches wide. The warriors and their families lived inside, where they cultivated bananas, sugar- cane, taro, and *kape* (giant taro). Thence they made frequent sorties against their enemies. To this day they dislike being united with the rest of the island, wishing only to be left alone to go their own way.

It may be that the Avatele people are the remnant of the aboriginal inhabitants, driven southward by Tongan immigrants, who have succeeded in impressing their language upon them. What they were, it is too late to speculate upon. The type is not Melanesian, though it has some Melanesian characteristics. There must have been other immigrants besides the Tongans. Drifts from the Gilbert Islands may have left a Micronesian trace in the blood, and from time to time there must have been arrivals from Aitutaki and other islands of the Cook Group, which lies to windward. Indeed, there is still a tradition of the wreck on the east side of the island of a canoe containing several men and one woman. The men were all killed, but the woman was kept as a wife. It may be that one of these arrivals was followed by an epidemic, and that the people took fright, and thereafter adopted their murderous system of quarantine.

There is more than one reason for believing that the island has been inhabited for five hundred years at least. Mr. Gill found the oldest historical tradition in Mangaia (I do not include mythological story) to be no older than four hundred and fifty years: the earliest tradition in Tonga is of about the same age; and, though Fornander professes to date Hawaiian history from far earlier, his methods seem to be too free to be convincing. Five centuries seem to be the limit which the memory of a people, unacquainted with writing, can attain, and the fact that the Niuéans have preserved no certain tradition of their origin seems to show that they were established as a race before that limit. Again, in Pylstaart Island, a known colony of Tongan castaways, a complete aristocracy on the complicated Tongan model was found in miniature, although the island is scarce a mile across. That the institutions of the Niuéans were republican suggests that they left Tonga before society in that group had crystallised into its present form. Moreover, so far from regarding the Tongans as brothers sprung from the same ancestors, the Niuéans had a traditional horror of them as "man-eaters," which by the way they were not. The tie must have been remote that allowed Polynesians to speak thus of their kinsmen, whatever injuries they had suffered at their hands. And lastly, though the Tongans, even as early as Tasman's visit in 1642, tattooed their thighs from the buttocks to the knees, tattooing was unknown in Niué until the arrival of the Samoan teachers.

Custom, of course, is more durable than tradition, and there was until lately a custom in Niué that is, I believe, unique in the history of the human race. When a boy was a few weeks old the old men assembled, and a feast was made. On the village square an awning of native cloth was rigged, and the child was laid upon the ground under it. An old man then approached it, mumbling an incantation, and performed the operation of circumcision in dumb-show with his forefinger. No child was regarded as a full-born member of the tribe until he had been subjected to this rite of *Matapulega*. Now, circumcision was pretty generally practised in Fiji, in Tonga, and in Samoa, but the Niuéans assert that the rite was never performed in their island except in this modified form. They even express disgust at the idea of such a mutilation, but they are quite unable to assign any reason for their own purposeless mummery. If what they say is true—and Mr. Lawes has no reason to doubt it—we have in this a perfect example of the survival of a meaningless form five centuries after the death of the custom that gave rise to it. In their old home the ancestors of the race practised circumcision, but, the operation being the prerogative of a skilled caste to which none of the band of castaways belonged, they did not dare to tamper with their children's bodies, nor yet to abandon a rite which their gods demanded.

There is a trace of totemism in certain animals being sacred to the people of certain villages; but these animals, at any rate in late heathen times, were not regarded as incarnations of the tutelary god. Thus, though Langa'iki was the god of Alofi, the owl (*lulu*), which was tabu to the same village, was not his incarnation. A small lizard, the *moko* (*Lawesii*), which is peculiar to the island, is sacred throughout Niué, and this must be the totem of the original castaways. I have already described how the soul of a dead man is supposed to have entered into the body of the first insect that crawls upon the cloth spread by the body: possibly the soul of some ancestor may have entered into the *moko* lizard in the same way, but it is more likely that the *moko* was a totem, and, if only Polynesian folklore were being systematically collected in all the Polynesian islands, we might, by comparing the Niuéans with other peoples to whom the *moko* is sacred, arrive at a clue to the origin of the people. In Fiji the bond known as *tauvu*—that is, the worship of the same god —has always been found to be a sign of a common origin, for the cult of the common ancestor is remembered long after the historical tradition of the division of the tribe has perished.

The Niuéans had a belief in a future state, albeit shadowy and ill-defined. The virtuous passed into *Aho-noa* (everlasting day), the vicious into *Po* (darkness), but there was none so bold as to conjecture what they did there. The virtues were kindness, courage in battle, chastity, theft from another tribe, the slaughter of an enemy; the vices, cowardice, the breaking of an agreement or a tabu, theft from a member of the tribe, homicide in the time of peace. Ardent Christians though they are, no effort of the missionary can avail to break them of their belief in the malevolence of ghosts, even of those who loved them best in life; the spirits of the dead seem compelled to work ill to the living without their own volition. And yet their malevolence may be directed into a seemly channel, for, though they cannot be summoned to answer the questions of the living, widows often go to the graves of their dead husbands and cry to them for help when they are oppressed, in the hope that they will afflict their oppressor with sickness. Even so did the Christian natives of a village in the Mathuata Province in Fiji when they rebelled against the government in 1895. To make their secession patent to the world they first killed and ate a village policeman, and then carried kava to the grave of their dead chief, imploring his assistance. The office of the priesthood (*Taula'atua*) was hereditary. And here is another curious survival of the customs of the original home. The kava plant (*piper methysticum*) abounds in Niué as in most other Polynesian islands; kava, as everybody knows, is the national drink of Polynesia; it was also the drink under which the priests went into their inspired frenzy. The Niuéans alone, of all the Polynesian races who know the use of kava, do not drink it as a beverage, reserving it for the inspiration of their priests. The Niuéan priests behaved much as priests do all the world over, that is to say, they took the offerings made to the gods as their perquisites. While they were in the frenzy of inspiration their voices were the voices of the god; at other times, though they had great influence, no special reverence was due to their persons. There were no built temples; the gods were approached under the open sky, as gods should be—upon consecrated mounds, or in sacred clearings in the forest. There was a perfect understanding between the priests and the petty chiefs, to their mutual advantage, for the chiefs could not afford to ignore the political influence of the priests, and the priests, knowing that a chief could invoke the god without their aid, realised that they were not indispensable.

The gods to whom offerings were made were the spirits of dead ancestors, for the gods of Polynesian myth were too remote to concern themselves with human affairs. Turner was informed in 1848 that a long time before they were wont to make offerings to an idol which had legs like a man, but that in the time of a great epidemic, believing that the sickness was caused by the idol, they broke it in pieces and threw it away.

Christianity has failed to eradicate the belief in witchcraft; indeed, in one curious particular, it has even strengthened it. As in Tonga and Fiji, when the perpetrator of a crime is undiscovered, it is common to summon the inhabitants of a village, and to require them each to swear upon the Book that he is not the guilty person. Sometimes the evildoer is discovered by the trembling of his hand; sometimes after taking the oath he falls sick from sheer fright and makes confession. In 1887 when I was in Lomaloma (Fiji) several cases of arson had occurred among the Tongans settled there. Mafi, the old native magistrate, caused every man and woman in the village to take the oath, and a week later he was summoned to a woman to receive her dying confession. As soon as she had relieved her conscience she began to mend, and she lived to take her trial for the crime. A very exalted personage in Tonga, in his anxiety to prove to me that he had had no relations with the French, a matter of which I had indubitable proof, called for a Bible, and would have imperilled his health in the same way had I not interfered. The custom, which probably originated with the early missionaries, has been disseminated far and wide throughout the Christianised Pacific by native teachers. So deeply rooted is it that all Mr. Lawes' efforts have failed to discourage it.

A common form of witchcraft was to take up the soil on which an enemy had set his footprint and carry it to a sacred place, where it was solemnly cursed in order that he might be afflicted with lameness. When preparing for war a piece of green kava was bound on either side of the spear-point to strike the enemy with blindness. Nowadays no spell can be more fatal than to imprison one of the sacred *moko* lizards in a bottle and bury it at the foot of a cocoanut tree with an appropriate curse, to destroy any person who may drink the water of the nuts. To ensure the working of this spell it was, of course, essential that the victim should come to know of his impending doom; a hint was enough to lay him on his bed from pure fright. There was one slender hope for him. Curses can be neutralised by counterspells and the voluntary imposition of tabus, such as abstaining from certain acts, or certain kinds of food, much as the ancient Hebrews laid themselves under vows. When other means fail, a knife is run into the nape of the patient's neck. It is not uncommon for medical officers in Fiji, when prescribing medicine for a patient, to be asked what *tabu* is to be observed, for most native medicine-men of repute insist upon certain prohibitions, such as abstention from all "red food" (*i.e.* shell fish, red *kaile*, roots, etc.), or from all food grown under the earth, as essential to the cure. If the victim of the spell believes in his own antidote he does not fall ill; if he is sceptical he sickens from fright; in either case the belief in witchcraft receives a gentle impetus.

No less active is the belief in the possession by evil spirits. Not long ago a middle-aged woman was hag-ridden. She rushed in frenzy about the country to the consternation and terror of the people, and for several days she neither ate nor slept. To one question only would she give a connected answer: she knew the name of the spirit that had entered into her. Knowing no means of exorcising him, the people let her alone, and she eventually recovered, having apparently no recollection of her seizure. Close beneath the phlegmatic surface of the Polynesian there runs a strong current of neurotic hysteria, often unsuspected by the Europeans that know them best. The early missionaries were startled at the frequent disturbance of their services by an outburst of frenzy on the part of their most promising converts, who professed to be possessed by the Holy Spirit as at Pentecost. They gabbled in an unknown tongue, while their neighbours patted them soothingly on the back to bring them back to their senses. It was nothing else than the inspired frenzy of the heathen priests, who shivered and foamed at the mouth, and squeaked in shrill falsetto when possessed by their god. To the same neurotic quality are to be ascribed that curious seizure described by Mr. Rathbone[9] among the Malays, known as Lâtë, where at the utterance of some simple word such as "cut" a man will spring to his feet and leap about in a frenzy, shouting "Cut! Cut! Cut!" in endless reiteration; and the curious affection known in Fiji as "Dongai," whereby two young people of a race not naturally amorous, being separated after a first cohabitation, will pine away and die from purely physical debility, or, as we should say, of a broken heart; and that strange surrender whereby a man who thinks himself bewitched will give up all hope of life, and will take to his mat and foretell correctly the hour of his death. In the early part of 1888 a young native private of the garrison stationed at Fort Carnarvon in Fiji fell sick on returning from furlough on the coast. His comrades soon discovered the cause: he had had one brief hour of happiness with the girl of his choice, her parents had discovered the liaison and had driven him from the village; they were both "dongai" and would surely die. Every means was taken to distract him, and I had just completed arrangements to send him down to the coast for change of air, when the camp blackguard, one Motulevote, had a seizure in the night, and woke up every man in the barrack-room. When asked whose spirit possessed him, he replied in a squeaky voice, "I am Avisai (the sick man). I am about to die. I shall die on Thursday." In the morning, it is scarcely necessary to say, Avisai, who had heard this cheering announcement, was too ill to move. When Motulevote appeared next morning among the defaulters in the orderly room, he treated himself as an interesting case, and was proceeding to give the fullest details of his symptoms when the remedy of the cane was prescribed. It was gravely explained to him that he personally was entitled to the greatest sympathy; it was imperative that his carcass should be made an uncomfortable lodging for wandering spirits, and that the strokes of the cane were intended to extend below the surface of his innocent skin to that of Avisai's truant spirit that lay within. It is said that the corporal who wielded the cane entered into the spirit of the cure, and when Motulevote howled, addressed himself to Avisai's spirit, who was reported to me as having fled at the tenth stroke. By adopting the same air of tender solicitude that nurses use towards a child after it has been made to take a dose of nauseous medicine, I believe that we ended by impressing Motulevote with a sense of obligation. At any rate the spirit took the hint and visited him no more, and Avisai ultimately recovered.

Cannibalism was unknown in Niué, which is remarkable in a Polynesian race destitute of animal food. This does not in itself entitle the people to rank high among Polynesian nations, for, as is well known, cannibalism is not inconsistent with considerable advance towards civilisation, and the absence of it may be found accompanied with a very low state of barbarism. The Hawaiians and the Maories, whose polity and art and ornate manners entitled them to be called semi-civilised, were cannibals; the South African bushmen were not. Nor did the Niuéans make human sacrifice, though infanticide used to be common in the cases of illegitimate children, or of children born in war time. In the latter case the child was disposed of by *fakafolau*; that is to say, the babies were laid in an ornamental basket cradle, and, with many tears, were set adrift upon the sea when the wind was off shore. Then, as now, mothers were very affectionate towards their children, and when stern necessity commanded this sacrifice, they had to be restrained by force.

CHAPTER VII

THE TRIBUNALS OF ARCADIA

HAPPY is the land that has neither taxes, nor treasury, nor paid civil service, nor prisons, nor police! The problem that puzzled Plato and Confucius and Machiavelli and Locke and Jeremy Bentham has never troubled Niué, for only once in its history has it felt the need of these things. It happened in 1887, when one Koteka slew his brother. He could not be acquitted—the man was disobliging enough to admit his guilt—the penal code had never contemplated such a crime as this. The chiefs sought counsel of Mr. Lawes, as they have ever done in moments of perplexity, and for once he was powerless to help them. There was no prison, and an execution carried out by natives was out of the question; the High Commissioner's Court in Fiji had no jurisdiction over natives, and the Pulangi Tau, or Council of War, that would have given the man short shrift in heathen days by telling off one of his judges to betray him into ambush, had long been dissolved. There was nothing for it but to sentence him to perpetual labour on the roads, and, as they could not sentence a free citizen to stand perpetual guard over him, they left it to the convict's honour to see that the sentence was carried out. But Koteka, who had showed singular callousness to the embarrassment of his fellow-countrymen, now came to their aid, which proved that there was good in the man, since he suffered little personal inconvenience from the sentence. A ship coming in a few weeks later, he boarded her without opposition, and worked his passage to Manahiki, where he is still living, to the undisguised relief of the native authorities.

The old criminal court was, as I have said, the Pulangi Tau, or Council of War, whose only rule of procedure was to meet and try the accused when he happened to be out of the way. The code was the Lex Talionis modified by the rank and influence of the defendant. Murder, that is the killing of a member of the tribe (for the slaying of a potential enemy was a virtue rather than a crime), was punished by the *kopega*. The trial was held in secret and without the knowledge of the accused. If he was condemned to death, some member of the court was told off to *afo* him, that is to say, to win his confidence by an open profession of friendship. The business of the executioner was thus drawn out into weeks. When he had wormed himself into his victim's confidence, a day was appointed, and a band of warriors was concealed at a concerted spot in the bush. Then the Judas, on the pretence of taking him to an assignation with some village beauty, led him into the ambush, and he was done to death by blows struck from behind. Adultery was punished by fine or by the paddle-club, according to the influence of the offender, and there were instances of persons being condemned to be the slaves of their accusers. The gratification of private revenge was recognised, and justice was administered capriciously, as must always be the case in a society that tolerates might as right.

All this was swept away by the five Samoan teachers. They brought with them the penal code of the London Missionary Society, which was already in full force in Tahiti and Rarotonga, and was beginning to displace the elaborate system of punishments in Samoa. When the Mission ship *Duff* sailed from Portsmouth the stocks were still in use, and just as they were being abandoned in England, they took root in the South Seas. But in 1859, as Dr. Turner records with complacency, the "Broom Road," which was to aid the good work by enabling the missionary to keep a horse, had become the sheet- anchor of the law. All malefactors, from thieves to truants from the Sunday school, were sentenced to a spell of work upon this road, calculated in fathoms according to the degree of their iniquity, and if at that early date it stretched already, as Dr. Turner says, from Avatele to Alofi, a distance of six miles, the greater part of the population must have brought themselves within the clutches of the law. In these days men must sin with greater impunity, for to keep the road in repair the entire male population is giving the first Monday in the month. On the very afternoon of my landing they took me with pride to see a gigantic feat of engineering on which they were engaged— nothing less than the grading of a steep hill of coral for wheel traffic, although the only carts in the island belong to the traders. A few charges of dynamite would have done the job in a week, but they were too proud to ask the white men to help them, and they had set about the task in the only fashion they knew, which was to light big fires on the limestone rock, and then break away the calcined surface with hammers, a few inches at a time. That bluff may be cut through some day, but it will not be in our time, nor in theirs.

The law courts of Niué have never felt the want of paid police. There is a judge in every village, who holds his court when and where he pleases, but preferably in the open air. A verbal summons is sent to the accused. If he appears, the trial proceeds, but if not, the court adjourns until such time as his contumacy yields to the constant worrying to which he is subjected. There are no particular rules of procedure. The great object is to get the accused to confess. Accuser and accused generally fall to wrangling before the judge, who sits quietly listening until they have done, when, having used this excellent opportunity for forming an opinion of the merits of the case, he pronounces sentence. When there is no clue to the perpetrator of a crime, it is not unusual for the judge to send for a Bible and solemnly curse him upon it. Then the real culprit generally falls ill from sheer fright, and confesses to save his life. Primitive as the system is, I feel sure, from my experience of the Tongan courts, that with more elaborate machinery the Niuéan magistrates will do less justice.

Three penalties are now recognised by the courts: the making of fifty or one hundred fathoms of road, the burning of an oven of lime, and the fine. The road-making consists in clearing the undergrowth, filling up the crevices in the jagged limestone with branch coral carried from the beach, and spreading a layer of sand over all. Making an oven of lime is supposed to take a fortnight— one week for cutting the firewood, and another for bringing coral to burn in the fire; but, inasmuch as there is no officer paid to see that the sentence is carried out, the courts have fallen into an easy way of imposing fines for all offences, which, being usually paid by the relations of the prisoner, are apt to fail as a deterrent.

It is not surprising that offences are on the increase. The abduction of married women to the bush—an offence that was kept down by the club in the old days—is a growing source of trouble. A fine paid by the relations of the co-respondent does not satisfy the injured husband, who might think his honour cleared if he could see the gallant sweating at labour on the public road. I remember once laying before the great Council of Chiefs in Fiji a proposal to substitute a civil action for damages for the criminal penalty for seduction. During the debate that followed not a single voice was heard in support of the proposal. The opinion was unanimous that the existing law was a safety-valve without which there would be constant explosions. A man wanted no monetary gain from his dishonour, and if he were denied the legitimate revenge of seeing the man that had injured him languishing in gaol, he would resort to the old remedy of the club. Suicide, which seems to have been common in heathen times, is still of not unfrequent occurrence. It is rarely committed deliberately, but in an access of rage or shame young men and women jump over the cliffs and are dashed to pieces on the coral rocks below. Like angry children, they are tempted to avenge themselves by picturing the trouble that they will bring upon the friends who have offended them.

Thefts from Europeans are settled in an informal manner that does credit to everyone but the thief. The European generally goes first to Mr. Lawes, who invites the chiefs to make inquiry. A Fono is held, and, as a rule, the offender is discovered. The honour of the island being concerned, the relations of the thief are obliged to make restitution, in some cases twofold. But even in cases where a close inquiry has failed to discover the thief, restitution is sometimes made by the district, even though the European has admittedly thrown temptation in the way of the thief by his own negligence. It was owing to the just and tactful arbitration of Mr. Lawes that the Europeans had no complaints to bring before me, and that there exists between the traders and the natives a good feeling that can scarcely be found in any other part of the Pacific. These good relations may not last. Mr. Lawes told me that the young bloods who have been abroad and have worked side by side with Europeans are becoming prone to be insolent and abusive to the traders, and that there is a disposition to take advantage of the traders' necessity when a copra ship is in by refusing to work for the time-honoured rate of a dollar a day. The Niuéan's mind does not deal in fractions; it works in dollars, and when one seems insufficient, it jumps lightly to two. "Two dollars or we strike," are the terms they spring upon the wretched trader, who knows that his ship cannot wait many hours in her dangerous anchorage, and that his copra may lie rotting in his sheds before another ship will come to take it. This is one of the questions that an English Resident may be trusted to deal with.

The judicial preference for moral suasion to overcome contumacy is shared by the Executive. Nothing is done in Niué without the decree of the Fono, a council attended by all the chiefs of villages and heads of families. The Fono is half parliament and half law-court. Nothing is too great or too small for its attention. Has a strong man encroached on a widow's yam patch, it is to the Fono that she makes her plaint. Has a villager of Avatele been rude to a visitor from Tuapa, it is to the Fono that he will be called to answer. Time was when the Fono made laws, but as the only copy of these enactments is in the possession of Mr. Lawes, and the magistrates have managed very well without them for many years past, legislation is a very rare part of its labours. It sometimes happens that a village has refused to obey the decree of the Fono. The Great Council flies into no vulgar passion, talks not of legal penalties, sets no police in motion. It simply announces that the next meeting will be held in the rebellious village. This means more than meets the eye, for councillors are hungry folk, and they do not bring sandwiches with them. No village would dare incur the odium of neglecting to feed its august visitors. The headstrong village knows its doom. Day after day the Fono will blandly hold its sittings, eating its meals with intervals of talk between, and one thing only will prorogue the session—the humble submission of its refractory entertainers. Is it surprising that no standing army is wanted to suppress sedition in Niué?

When I asked to see the Statute Book, Mr. Lawes, who combines with his other unofficial functions the duties of Custos Rotulorum, produced a faded sheaf of foolscap paper. It was the only existing copy of the Acts of King Fataäiki, and it was doubtful whether any of the magistrates, who administered the code from memory, knew of its existence. It was simple in the extreme. Theft and adultery were to be punished with labour on the roads; for traffic in strong liquor and the sale of land, both absolutely forbidden, no penalties were provided. I would fain have left the law in its nebulous and elastic condition had it not been for the increasing proneness of the Niuéan to remove his neighbour's landmark and—if the naked truth be told—his neighbour's wife. Having with me the Penal Code which I drafted for the Tongans in 1891, I dictated to Mr. Lawes the simplest and the shortest Penal Code that every nation had, providing broadly for every crime in the calendar, with penalties ranging from a fine of a plaited straw hat to a maximum of six months' labour on the roads. The omission was criminal assault upon children —a crime unknown in Niué, Mr. Lawes assured me, though by a strange coincidence, as I heard afterwards, this very crime was committed within a month from the passing of the code. My part of the work was finished in two hours, and I blushed when I accepted the offer of my patient amanuensis to make the translations and fair copies after my departure, and even to persuade King Tongia to the task of commending it to his council—the only legislative body. To quote Mr. Lawes' own words, written six weeks afterwards: "We got the Quarantine Regulations through at Fono on May 1st. At the same time I read the translation of the laws which you wrote out, and suggested that the present would be a fitting time to revise their laws, and, together with those left by you, get all written out and put in force. The proposal was received more cordially than I expected. The *patus* had two sittings at Alofi. In every case in which they had similar laws to those left by you they voted for the *mena fou* in preference to the old. I wrote out all on which they were unanimous, and at the Fono at Tuapa to-day they have passed them by show of hands, and got the king's signature affixed. The late king was an intelligent, shrewd man, but I could not get him to do what Tongia has now done. There was a little hesitation in substituting work in almost every case for fines. The constables shrugged their shoulders at six or three months on the roads, and no pay. We advised them to pass the law and arrange afterwards about some remuneration for constables. For feeding the prisoners for the longer terms of labour they have agreed to let them off two days a week, to work for themselves and get food. In addition to fines, they have decided upon a sixpenny poll-tax per annum for man and wife and sons up to the age of going away in ships: unmarried women and girls exempt. The beginning of taxes in Savage Island! What will it grow to?"

There was one other matter in which I was obliged to tamper with legislation. There were cases of bubonic plague in Australia and New Zealand, and ships were free to communicate with the shore at four different parts of the coast. A master might even land his sick on the island and sail away unchallenged if he chose, and though masters who would commit such an act of infamy are fortunately rare in these days, the risk of infection was too great to be left unprovided for. There being no Customs officer or medical man on the island, it was obvious that nothing could be done without the willing cooperation of the Europeans. The nine traders responded to my invitation to a meeting. Having laid before them the risk the island ran, I called for volunteer health officers. It was first proposed that Alofi should be made the only port of entry, but to this it was objected that masters, having anchored at one port, would refuse to incur the delay of going on to another and returning before they began to discharge their cargo. There was nothing for it but to appoint a health officer for every port, and to the credit of the gentlemen present volunteers at once came forward. Quarantine Regulations were drafted to be passed by the native council (which must have been sorely puzzled by the unaccustomed phraseology); the health officers undertook to board every incoming vessel, and demand the Bill of Health, at the same time serving upon the master a copy of the penalties he would incur if he allowed men to land before he got pratique; and King Tongia, for his part, undertook to punish any native who should put off to a vessel flying the yellow flag. It was a game of bluff—for how was the penalty of £50 or six months' imprisonment to be enforced?—but it served its purpose.

CHAPTER VIII

A NATIVE ENTERTAINMENT

IT was not in accordance with Niuéan custom that visitors should go away empty-handed. At three o'clock one sunny afternoon we were summoned to an entertainment on the square of grass before the Mission-house. Sitting with our backs to the gate, we faced a grassy stage, built, as it were, of palm trees—their stems for wings, their feathery, glistening fronds for flies, and for background the blue Pacific clear to the horizon, save for the *Porpoise* lying at anchor below.

First there came a band of shy girls with garlands twined in their black tresses and presents in their hands, shepherded by a few armed warriors (in coat and trousers, be it confessed) and three or four aged women capering grotesquely. Sitting down in two double rows facing one another, they began to chant pæans in our honour to the cadence of an English drum. Mr. Lawes, sitting at my elbow, translated as they sang. It must be confessed that both in voice and melody they fell far behind the Samoans and the Tongans, but a people who in a single night can compose and teach to a chorus of fifty persons words and music, with the accompanying gestures, is not lightly to be called unmusical. One of the songs described the hoisting of the flag; the girls imitated the action of hauling on a rope and the salute fired from the ship as they sang *"Fusi! Fusi!"* ("Pull up! Pull up!"). Viewed in a body like this, the women were not prepossessing. Their straight, greasy-looking black hair, fat cheeks, ill-shaped features, and clumsy figures wanted more than a good-natured expression and bright smiles to redeem them from ugliness. The songs were led by the composer, a daughter of the late king and sister to the young gentleman who had acted as our pilot, an enormously fat girl, with a smile that seemed to lose itself behind her ears. After the singing had been protracted into the second half-hour the old gentleman of the nautical uniform, whom we had nicknamed "the Admiral," broke in upon the stage to expostulate. It appeared that he too had a band of singers behind the scenes, and that the first choir was cheating him of his fair share of our attention. He had now discarded his ancient beaver for a homemade cocked hat, hastily constructed in imitation of mine. At his remonstrance the first choir good- naturedly yielded him place, which meant that every member of the troupe came up to us in turn, presenting us with some trinket with the left hand and shaking hands with the right. The pile of presents between our feet rose higher and higher, and the garlands wreathed our knees until we looked too Bacchanalian for the gravity of the crowd of blue-jackets who were looking on. There were fans and shells and coloured pebbles, and crab shells with scarlet spots upon them, and tail feathers of the frigate bird, and live chickens bound fast by the leg, and necklaces of little yellow shells, which, as we afterwards found, are highly prized in Tonga.

THE KING AND QUEEN TAKE THEIR SEATS

The man on the right is armed with both spear and paddle-club

The Admiral's troupe now advanced upon the stage, and we were again reminded that dignity is little accounted of in Niué. At its head capered the Admiral and three old ladies, and warriors with spears in poise danced awkwardly in the rear. While the song was in progress the Admiral's sister, a dame as old as himself, danced before us in a flame-coloured nightgown. No stately measure was this, but a vulgar caper of the Moulin Rouge that recked not of singers or of drum-beat. With her fists clenched on a level with her ears, this weird old person pranced solemnly in the background until she wore down the other dancers and was left to caper by herself. When flesh and blood would bear no more, she sat down panting beside us. Blown though she was, she had no intention of yielding the *crachoir* to the legitimate performers, for now she called for a wooden drum, upon which she beat vigorously for a few minutes quite out of time to the music. Then, flinging it aside, she whipped a nose-flute from the bosom of her nightgown, and blew soft notes upon it with one nostril, watching us the while out of the corner of her eye, lest our attention should stray from her. Whatever further tricks she had to show us were cut short by the close of the singing and the consequent handshaking, in which she gravely took her part, presenting me with her nose-flute. Her buffoonery did not provoke a smile from the other performers until they noticed our amusement, when some of the girls smiled indulgently upon her. It is possible that she was touched in the head, though Mr. Lawes had always known her as a staid matron and a regular attendant at church. We were told that this dance of old women, which is practised, so far as I know, in no other part of Polynesia, and which Mr. Lawes had never seen, was a revival of an ancient custom.

The warriors now engaged in mimic duel. A short man brandishing a paddle-club with both hands challenged another armed with a spear. Contorting his features into the most horrible grimaces, the club man rushed upon his antagonist, and appeared to be on the point of cracking his skull, when he seemed to take alarm at the spear and retired step by step before the other's onset. Thus by alternate rushes the fight swayed to and fro, until both the duellists were out of breath and gave place to others. The feints were so cleverly done that more than once I feared for a moment that they had lost their heads in the excitement, and that one or the other would receive a dangerous wound. What they must have looked in war paint, with tangled locks over their eyes and matted beards chewed between their teeth, it was easy to imagine, and I think that the success of the performance, which was so popular that we had to interfere when we had had enough of it, was due to the fact that it was not play-acting at all, but actual warfare as it was waged in the old days; for, as I shall presently explain, there is good reason to believe that hand-to-hand fighting was seldom more than a series of feints persisted in until the weaker vessel ran away, leaving his antagonist master of the field.

When the dancers had withdrawn a man rose from the ring of spectators and began an oration of welcome. He was the headman of Avatele, and it soon became evident that the headmen of each of the eleven villages intended to deliver themselves of the oratory of which I had defrauded them when the Treaty was signed. Mr. Lawes achieved the difficult feat of interpreting in a rapid undertone without interrupting the speakers, whose fluency and declamation would shame the average public speaker in England. The fact is that you will scarcely find in the Pacific a native who cannot make a fair speech in public on any subject at a moment's notice. There is none of the hesitation, the tiresome reiteration, the halting delivery, and the dependence upon the rhetorical conjunction "er-er-er" when the reservoir of thought runs dry, that distinguish the efforts of the male Briton who is called suddenly to his feet. (I say *male* Briton because I have been given to understand that the oratory of platform ladies, having none of these defects, is a pure delight to listen to.) The Polynesian is never at a loss for a word, for a phrase, or for an illustration. He owes, perhaps, something to his language, for I am not the only Englishman who finds it easier to make a speech in a Polynesian language than in English.

Niué, lying east of the 180th degree of longitude, keeps western time, and our

Sunday was the natives' Saturday. Captain Ravenhill, in compliance with my hint that the natives should have none but pleasant recollections of our visit, allowed no one to go on shore who was below the rank of petty officer. I do not think that, if he had, the result would have been different, for after six weeks' stay in Tonga, where every man on board was allowed the usual shore leave, the king assured me that the *Porpoise's* was the best-behaved ship's company that had ever visited his kingdom. But the British petty officers are a class apart, and if I were set the task of winning the confidence of suspicious and hostile natives, I should ask for an escort of the first naval petty officers that came to hand and consider the work done. On returning from a walk late in the afternoon we heard sounds of merrymaking in the village square, and found the whole population sitting convulsed with laughter at an entertainment provided by their visitors. It appeared that the shore party, returning to their boat, had discovered a band of urchins playing catch with oranges, and seized upon the opportunity for teaching the new British subjects the British national game. With sticks for wickets and cocoanut butts for bats, they soon had the game going, and when we came up a boy of eight was bowling to a bearded engine-room artificer, who was going through the antics of clown-cricket to the huge delight of the onlookers. The little boys positively wept when the boat came to carry away their new-found friends.

As no one has yet done justice to the enormous political influence wielded by English blue-jackets in these seas, I will here set down an unwritten chapter of history, related to me by the King of Tonga, in His Majesty's own words:—

"I think that it is because the English joke with us Tongans that they are our friends. Now, when the *Taulanga* (H.M.S. *Tauranga*) was here, there was a marine who used to carry the letters to the post-office. He could not speak our language, yet he spent much time with my guard-boys in the guard-room at the end of the wharf, and was beloved of them. One day another man-of-war was signalled. She was the flagship of the French admiral, and we all watched through telescopes, wondering whether the two ships would salute one another, and whether the French admiral would first call upon the English captain, or the English captain would first call upon the admiral, for we thought that the first to call would acknowledge himself to be the inferior of the other. And while we watched, a boat put off from the *Taulanga* to carry the captain to the French ship; therefore some said, 'See, the Englishman admits his inferiority.' But they did not speak thus on the next day. It was a Sunday, and the French sailors, to the number of about eighty, landed in boats, and marched to the Roman Catholic church at Maofanga to attend the service. The English marine was in the guard-room when they passed, and the Tongan guard-boys jested with him, saying how fine the Frenchmen looked and how terrible they must be in battle, at which the marine spat upon the ground, but said nothing, and presently he went away to walk in the town. About noon the sentry called the guard to the door, saying, 'Here come the Frenchmen!' and while they watched them marching proudly in lines of four, they saw also their friend, the English marine, coming down a cross-road from the town, so that he must encounter the Frenchmen at the place where the two roads met, though as yet he saw them not because of the trees. 'Now,' they said, 'we shall see an Englishman abashed, for our friend loves not the French, and when he comes upon these suddenly, he will turn and slink back into the town as white clergymen of rival churches are used to do when they encounter one another in the street.' But they were false prophets, for as soon as their friend saw the Frenchmen he threw back his head proudly and stepped high, behaving like a general about to lead his troops into battle. So waited he at the cross-road, and when they had come up to him he put himself at their head, and marched so bravely in his red coat, that the Tongans cried out, 'Lo, a king is approaching us with his bodyguard! It behoves us to salute him with all humility!' The face of the French officer was not good to look upon, for when he called upon his men to stamp the ground and let the marine go on, he also stamped the ground, and when they pressed forward to pass him he quickened his steps and kept with them, as if he was indeed their leader. Nor was it better when they passed the guard-room, and saw even the Tongan sentry dissolved in laughter, for the marine behaved as if he was too exalted to know his friends, save for a secret sign that he made to them with one eyelid. So they went on together to the boat. The rumour of this thing was carried throughout Tonga, and the people thought more of this marine than of the French admiral and all his men."

When I read the narratives of Captain Cook and John Williams, the missionary, I believed the Niuéans to be the most ferocious warriors that the world has ever seen. Now I have my doubts. The sham duel performed in our honour at Alofi was no doubt a very terrifying performance, and to witness, as Williams did, an old gentleman of sixty in a state of nature, smeared with charcoal, with a long grey beard plaited into rats'-tails, poising and quivering his spear, distorting his features most horribly by distending his mouth, gnashing his teeth, and forcing his eyeballs almost out of their sockets, "thrusting his long grey beard into his mouth, and gnawing it with the most savage vengeance," and maintaining throughout the performance a loud and hideous howl, must have made a lasting impression. And King Tongia, it is true, could talk of little less than the warlike exploits of himself and his fathers. But one of His Majesty's anecdotes has left me to wonder whether Niuéan warfare often overstepped the limits of beard-chewing. He was relating how an ancestor of his, the greatest warrior the world has known, met the second greatest warrior in single combat. The battle-light glowed in

Tongia's left eye as he described the weapons, the strength, the courage, and the ferocious aspect of the warriors. At his recital the stoutest heart must have quailed. But noticing that the battlefield of this historic duel was no larger than the dining-room of a suburban villa, and knowing that only one of them could have come alive from a combat in so confined a space, Mr. Lawes inquired which of them was killed. "Oh, neither!" said the king, and passed lightly to other battle stories. I believe that in Niué the battle was not to the strong, but to the ugly. Your object in battle was not so much to crack your opponent's skull as to frighten him off the field, and if your grimaces and howls failed to make him run, you knew that he meant business, and you ran away yourself. If you could make up well, you became a *toa* (brave), and the ball was at your feet, for the *toa* ruled their rulers, made and unmade kings, and lived on the fat of the land. We have no photographs of the famous men of old, but I suspect that they were blessed from birth with a natural uncomeliness which they fostered with art, by plaiting their beards into rats'- tails, and by assiduous practice of the battle-howl. That a whole people should devote itself to the cult of ugliness is, I think, uncommon even among the most primitive races. Nearly every warlike people do something to "make-up" for the part of a warrior, but their object is to strike fear into their enemies by an effect of noble and awful dignity. The Samoans don a lofty headdress; the Fijians disguise themselves with black and white paint; the people of New Britain wear masks. The Aztecs and the Mallicolo Islanders, it is true, compress their skulls to a point, and the Maories disfigure their faces with tattooing, but only because what we regard as disfigurements minister to their ideas of beauty. With the sole exception of the Niuéans the Polynesian races never forget their dignity so far as to make themselves either ludicrous or grotesque. In the whole island of Niué I saw but one man with a trace of dignity about him, and he was a Samoan teacher. As for the rest, from the grey-bearded elder to the smallest child, they all behaved like schoolboys. Some alien strain in the blood has debased a race of Polynesian aristocrats into Melanesian republicans.

The loss of life from warfare can never have been great. I imagine that in place of desperate assaults upon fortified strongholds, as in Tonga and New Zealand, the Niuéan warrior contented himself with cutting off defenceless stragglers and slaying individuals by ambush. Naturally timorous, the Niuéans did not even dare to execute their criminals honestly.

Their arms did not lend themselves to precision. The paddle-club was almost as ineffective a weapon as an oar, for, being flimsy and light, the blade caught the air, and the force of the stroke was diminished. The spear was a mere stick sharpened at one end, and, as we have seen, the warrior who launched one at Cook at five yards range failed to hit him. If the slings and the hand-grenades fashioned from the cave-stalactites, rounded and polished, had been accurate in aim, scarce a man of Cook's party would have escaped. But the club and the spear were excellent weapons for brandishing, and scaring the enemy was all that the Niuéan warrior aimed at. The Fijians, who are often quoted as types of ferocity, expended their heroism in the preliminary *mbole*, or "boasting," before they encountered the enemy. Striking the earth with his club before his chief, one cries, "I cause the earth to tremble; it is I who meet the enemy to-morrow!" Another, swinging his club, shouts, "This club is a defence, a shade from the heat of the sun and the cold of the rain; you may come under it!" But in the face of an enemy who will not run away the performance fell short of the promise, and the frontal attack was unknown unless a contingent of Tongans happened to be of the party. I have never myself witnessed a fight between two war parties of natives armed with nothing but their own weapons, but a European, the late Mr. English, who saw one in Cloudy Bay, British New Guinea, thus described it to me. One party having been pursued on to the open beach made a stand, whereupon the pursuers halted, uncertain what to do. The pursued, taking heart, shouted their battle-cry and made a move towards them; the others ran back for fifty yards or so, and rallied in their turn. This bloodless see-saw having continued for three or four rounds, accompanied by much abusive language, the battle ended by the invaders taking to flight. Never once did either side get within spear-throw of the other, though spears enough flew harmlessly into the sand.

This dislike of hard knocks is a provision of Nature for perpetuating island races. Were it otherwise, how could an island thirteen miles by four continue to be populated? With pigs, women, and land to quarrel about, a race of warriors cooped up within such narrow limits would be reduced to a single survivor in less than a century.

CHAPTER IX

BYWAYS OF CUSTOM

A MONG those who had made speeches to us after the dancing was the headman of Hakupu village, whose features had been destroyed by the ravages of lupus. The roof of his mouth being also involved, his speech was hardly intelligible even to Mr. Lawes. "I am afflicted, as you see," he said, "yet could I not bear to let this day pass without bidding you welcome to Niué-Fekai." I questioned Mr. Head about the diseases of the natives. He said that yaws (Frambæsia, so called from the strawberry-like appearance of the eruption), and phthisis, coughs and colds were quite unknown before the arrival of the Samoan teachers. The people, when he first arrived on the island, generally died of old age. The diseases of that time were *makulokuli*, an urinary trouble, lupus and scrofula. Since intercourse with ships has become common, there has been ample justification for the policy that earned for the Niuéans from Cook the title of Savage Islanders. Nowadays every child has yaws as a matter of course, though, being a contagious disease, it might easily be stamped out by isolation. Whooping- cough has never left the island since its introduction. Measles, brought in two years ago by a labourer returning from abroad, occasioned about one hundred deaths, but though it lasted twelve months, so efficient was the native quarantine of infected villages that Tuapa escaped it altogether. The worst form of contagious disease, unknown thirty-four years ago, is said now to be common in the tertiary stage, especially among infants. As its name, *tona Tahiti* (Tahitian yaws), implies, it was introduced from Tahiti during the sixties. There is not much ophthalmia, and deformities are rare. There are a few cases of insanity—our friend, the Admiral's sister, is fast qualifying to rank among them—and the people do not treat them kindly.

Serious illness is still regarded as possession by the spirit of some dead person, and a necessary part of the treatment is to evict the spirit in possession. I have already told how a mother destroyed her daughter's grave by fire in order to burn the spirit that was afflicting her. Nearly all the old women are medical practitioners. The number of herbal decoctions that they administer to a sick person is incredible. If one fails in working a cure before their eyes, they administer another, and if the patient persists in dying after drinking them all, as is not uncommon, they lay the blame upon the spirit, and their practice suffers no injury. The best known of these native doctors exact heavy fees in kind for their services, but their faith in their own nostrums must be rather slender, for they themselves, when taken ill, resort to the

Mission dispensary. Mr. Lawes and Mr. Head, who both dispense medicines for the natives, are agreed in finding that the natives are more susceptible to the action of drugs than Europeans, and require smaller doses.

From a photograph by   *J. Martin,*
Auckland.

A GRAVE IN TONGA

Made of coral, white sand, and polished black pebbles. The garlands worn by friends are suspended above as a mark of affection

Families are large. Five or six children are quite common, and there is more than one woman now alive who has given birth to sixteen children. There used to be no barren women, though now childless women are not unknown. These generally adopt children, whom they treat with the same affection as if they had borne them. The marriage of first cousins is not popular as in Fiji, though there is a trace of the sentiment that has produced the curious custom of concubitancy practised by the Fijians. The offspring of two sisters are absolutely forbidden to marry, but the children of two brothers, or of a brother and sister, may do so without shocking the sentiments of the community. In the case of the offspring of two sisters the prohibition dates from a time when a man who married one member of a family had a right to marry all her sisters, and it was never certain that the children of sisters had not the same father. The population of 4,576, as will be seen in the returns in the appendix, is now stationary.

Relationships are traced back for four or five generations. The people seem to be in a transition state between Patriarchy and Matriarchy. A grown-up son inherits his father's house and land, but the daughters seem to have claims upon their mother's brother, and though these claims are universally recognised, there is nothing approaching the extraordinary rights of the Fijian *vasu*.

The land is the common property of the septs, represented by their heads. The present boundaries are not of old standing, for in fighting times the braves (*toa*) ignored all rights, and seized upon any land they thought themselves strong enough to hold, and some of this spirit still survives. But there is land enough for all and to spare, and the junior members of a sept come to their laird whenever they are in need of land to plant on. There is individual ownership in a sense, because a title can be acquired by cultivation, and the sons inherit their father's land; but no landowner can demise his holding to anyone outside the limits of his sept, and, in default of heirs, the land reverts to the head of the sept for assignment to other members of it. The headman receives a sort of rent in the form of labour and produce, and the firstfruits, formerly offered to the gods, are sometimes presented to him. Last year the Pacific Islands Company applied for a lease of two hundred acres in the interior for a plantation, and as there were no native plantations on the land, they considered that the refusal of their application was due to mere obstruction. As King Tongia had laid great emphasis upon one of his laws which prohibited the sale of land to foreigners, I thought it possible that he did not understand the difference between a lease and a sale, and I was at some pains to explain that the company was not asking him to do anything contrary to the spirit of the law. But he replied that the refusal rested upon other grounds. The persons who had expressed their willingness to lease were in fact not the exclusive owners. Every member of several different septs would claim a voice in granting the lease, and the boundaries of this unoccupied land were so ill-defined that the division of the rent would lead to endless bickering and dispute. Moreover it might well happen that the poorer members of some of the septs would be left landless, on the excuse that the lease of so large an area had eaten up the land for which they might have applied. He satisfied me that the boundaries would have to be settled by some sort of commission before it would be prudent to grant leases for plantations.

Like all the Polynesians, the Niuéans are possessed by an earth-hunger that nothing will satisfy. Most of the jealousy between villages has its root in land disputes, and the land question is daily becoming more complicated through the system that allows titles to be acquired by cultivation, because the entanglements can no longer be cut periodically by the sword, or rather by the paddle-shaped club. The planting of plantains or of yams by leave of the owner confers no title, but the planting of cocoanuts and other fruit trees does so. In Fiji it is not uncommon for one man to own the land and another the trees growing upon it, but in Niué the trees carry the land with them. Thus, there being no boundary marks, encroachment by tree-planting is a continual source of friction. It presses particularly hard upon widows and orphans, whose protests against tree-planting are unheeded, and who are frequently robbed of land inherited from their dead husbands and fathers in this way. The excuse usually given for this injustice is that widows and orphans are in wrongful possession, for their connection with the dead man's sept ceases with his death, and they should go back to their own kin for land to plant on; but that this argument is regarded as sophistry is shown by the fact that the majority of natives condemn the practice.

I have purposely refrained from touching on the flora and fauna of Niué because they are subjects that are better left by the passing traveller to the specialist, who is certain sooner or later to visit so promising a field as a solitary island originally destitute of domestic animals. Unlike human customs, which change with the old order, the fauna of an island is not affected by the fictions of human statecraft; the birds and the lizards and the land-shells will continue to breed their kind under the Union Jack as they did when the Pulangi Tau swayed the destinies of Niué-Fekai. But I must make an exception in favour of the *Musca Domestica*, the common house-fly. All the later visitors agree in describing the swarms of flies as an Egyptian plague. The bodies of the men who came off the ships were black with them, and I knew of them by reputation long before we arrived at the island. We were prepared for the worst when our royal pilot boarded us, and we were astonished to find that he came on board unattended. One of our first questions was, "Where are your flies?" and we found that the Europeans on shore shared our surprise. At Christmas, 1899, they had been as bad as ever: then came February and March, unusually wet months, and the flies entirely disappeared. During our stay not a fly was seen. Those are the facts: entomologists must explain them. The house-fly, as most people know, takes something under fourteen days from the laying of the egg to the hatching of the pupa. The voracious larvæ are supposed to earn their living by scavenging, but the Niuéans have dispensed with their services for some months without being one penny the worse. Their satisfaction will be short- lived: a new breed will be introduced by the steamers, and Niué will be fly- blown again.

CHAPTER X

WESTWARD HO!

T HE following day was the Niué Sunday. It had been my intention to sail soon after daybreak, but Mr. Lawes seemed to be so anxious that we should attend the morning service that I agreed. It seems that the influence of the Mission is waning from a variety of causes. Chief among these is the passion for foreign travel, which, having been the cause of the peopling of these remote spots, still possesses all the natives of the smaller Polynesian islands. Every year numbers of young men return from abroad and disturb the still waters of the island with fascinating tales of the emancipation of foreign lands, where men get drunk and swear and break the Sabbath with impunity. They play upon the mercantile instinct of the old men with garbled stories, told them by beachcombers, of the money that the missionaries make out of the natives. Every year Mr. Lawes, who has devoted thirty years' unremitting labour to these people, finds arrayed against him a growing opposition composed of all the "bad hats" in the island.

The church was crowded. We were placed with the other Europeans within a sort of chancel rail, facing the congregation, who sat on the matted floor. Seven-eighths at least were women, whose enormous straw hats, heavily trimmed with artificial flowers, resembled a vast flower bed. Here and there a dusky face and a pair of bright eyes peeped out, but behind the first two rows stretched an unbroken area of hat brim, like a light-coloured soil in which the flowers were growing. From the roots of the bed proceeded a whimpering chorus of babies, and every now and then, when a louder burst threatened to drown the voice of the preacher, officials stationed at intervals round the walls stirred the flowers at the noisiest spot with a long pole. Then a woman would rise, producing from among her petticoats a jolly fat baby, who instinctively threw his legs apart in the proper position for straddling his mother's back, while she threw a folded cloth over her shoulders as a sling for him to sit in. He would then smile complacently at us as he was carried out, as who should say, "I have won my point; I advise you to howl too." Babies flowed out all through the sermon, but there was little cessation of the overtone of whimper. At the end of the sermon Mr. Lawes announced that the ship was leaving, and that it was not improbable that a salute might be fired. This, he explained, must not be accounted to us for unrighteousness; a ship belonging to the Queen was no Sabbath-breaker. It was simply a matter of the calendar, because the ship, coming from a far land, reckoned its days differently, and counted the Niuéan Sabbath a Monday. If anyone in that great congregation remembered the petty officers' clown cricket on what was the ship's Sabbath, they did not show it.

Shaking hands is better than rubbing noses, but that is all that can be said for it, for, where two Niuéans of the old time rubbed noses, one hundred insist upon shaking hands. Every male of the congregation approached us in unending file at the church door to indulge in this friendly exercise, and, thinking that this was to pass for our farewell, we had not the heart to escape. Were I made Resident of the island, the first bill that I would introduce to the Fono would be a "Bill for Abolishing the Pernicious Custom of Hand-shaking" (short title, "The Salutations Act, 1901"). It would contain a single clause substituting for contact with the hands a vulgar nod, with the optional addition of the word "Alofa!" on pain of being sentenced to shake the handle of the village pump until the village reservoir was full. But legislation in such matters is not invariably successful even in Tonga, the most overgoverned community in the world. The ancient form of salutation to superiors in Tonga was to drop everything that you were carrying and to crouch at the roadside with the head sunk between the knees. When the country, under the guiding hand of its Wesleyan pastors, set out to seek *fakasivilaise* (which is "civilisation"), and decreed it "to be the will of God that man should be free, as He has made all men of one blood," some modification was felt to be necessary. King George Tubou I. himself settled the point in his fine autocratic manner. His subjects, high and low alike, were to exchange greetings by raising the hand perpendicularly from the elbow about six inches from the right ear— an invention of His Majesty's own, suggesting a compromise between a friendly wave of the hand and a military salute. And, having noticed that the natural cheek of the Tongan swelled mountainously when he could look down upon his fellows from the saddle, he further decreed that men should dismount from their horses when they encountered the person or passed the house of any member of his House of Lords. Ten years ago, while he lived, you might have seen his decree in daily practice in the streets of Nukualofa; now Jack has grown so much better than his master that all outward marks of deference have passed away, men jostle their chiefs openly in the road, good manners and respect for authority have perished with their outward symbols, and the only person in whose presence a Tongan lays aside his jaunty swagger is a mounted policeman. A fine of one dollar or four days' imprisonment still frowns upon the disrespectful from the pages of the statute book, but the noble loses dignity by prosecuting, while the policeman gains promotion.

At the Mission House the last box was being packed, and, despite our entreaties, Mrs. Lawes was generously stripping her house of all her curiosities as parting gifts—shells, rare mats, barbaric ornaments and specimens of ingenuity in plaiting. If the boat had not been lying in jeopardy among the rocks below, there would have been nothing left on her walls or in her cabinets. This lavish bounty was to be the impression we were to carry away from this delightful island, wherein we had been overwhelmed with a hospitality that we can never repay, and with a kindness that we shall never forget. The path to the landing-place was lined with our native friends pressing forward for a parting hand-clasp. Down we scrambled to the boat, which rose and fell with the swell between two walls of jagged coral; we were afloat again, the features of our friends waving to us from the landing-place grew blurred and indistinct, the three-pounders banged, we were off. In a few minutes H.M.S. *Porpoise* was dipping her nose into the swell, the island was fading into a grey haze on the horizon, and it was difficult to believe that we had not dreamed the whole adventure.

It has been a year of high emotion for Niué-Fekai. Six weeks later—on June 1st—the *Tutunekai*, a steam yacht belonging to the New Zealand Government, brought Mr. Seddon, the Premier of New Zealand, who, while cruising for the sake of his health, was occupied with his scheme of federating the Pacific Islands under New Zealand.

On October 19th—six months to a day from the date of our landing—H.M.S. *Mildura* arrived with Lord Ranfurly, Governor of New Zealand, to proclaim the formal annexation of the island.

The natives must be sorely puzzled by the solemn pageant of flag-hoisting, for the Protectorate Jack was hauled down, and a counterpart of it run up in its stead with the usual salutes. The deed of cession was signed, like the treaty, in the school-house, two villages, Alofi and Avatele, dissenting, until they saw that they were to be outvoted by the other nine. There are, it seems, even in Niué a few professional grumblers, who accused King Tongia and his chiefs of having sold the country to a foreign power, and even went so far as to attack Mr. Lawes for having acted as interpreter at the proclamation of the Protectorate. The ringleader had come to my meeting primed with a hostile speech, but, having been denied an opportunity for unburdening himself, he discharged it upon the next meeting of the Fono. He was busy organising opposition to Lord Ranfurly, when, in an unlucky moment for his cause, he was called up to sign the deed of cession as the representative of Avatele. Thus was he impaled on the horns of a dilemma. If he refused, another would have gone down to posterity as a greater than he in his own village; if he accepted, he stultified his own words. Staggered by the compliment, or reflecting, perhaps, that it is the written word that endures, he cast his principles to the winds and signed the deed. That is the last that we shall hear of the Home Rulers of Niué.

My readers will rejoice to hear that King Tongia is not to suffer the mortification of parting with the title for which he worked so hard. Filtered through His Majesty's peculiar cast of mind this part of the agreement may not be without embarrassment to the new Resident. So far from suffering any eclipse, Tongia emerges from the late events with an added dignity, according to his rendering of the clause that refers to him in the agreement, "It has pleased the two of us, Me and Victoria ..." (*Kua metaki ko e tokoua a maua, Ko au mo Vitoria*). To do him justice, I think that if he had been offered the alternative between abdicating unconditionally with a life pension, or continuing to enjoy his high title without emolument, he would have taken the pension; but, since that temptation was never put in his way, he is quite right to cling to what he has. And who shall grudge him this modest satisfaction? As Mr. Gladstone once said of Peel, "I should not say that he was egotistical, but I should say that his own personality occupied no inconsiderable area in his mental vision." There are worse men and weaker kings than Tongia of Niué-Fekai.

The future of this interesting little people depends upon the man chosen by the New Zealand Government to be the first Resident. A wise, sympathetic, and patient man, endowed with a sense of humour, not over-sensitive about his dignity, and content to gain his point by suasion rather than pressure, will be able to do what he pleases with the people; a pompous or choleric person will have the island about his ears before he has been there a month. New Zealand has not always been wise in her choice of residents for her dependencies, though no colony has better material to choose from. During the next few years she will be on her trial: if she governs her new dependencies wisely, keeping out the liquor traffic, and fostering the prosperity and contentment of her native fellow-subjects, she may prove herself fit to be entrusted with the government of a great South Sea confederation; but if she uses her new dependencies merely as a means of rehabilitating her declining South Sea trade, and is cynically indifferent to the interests of the natives, she will find herself with a new and more difficult Native Question on her hands, and her great scheme will be rudely shattered. In her own interest, therefore, besides that of the sturdy, energetic little people that she has taken under her wing, she will pray for a wisdom in her second experiment of governing natives that was sadly wanting in her first.

As I began this account of the island with a letter from one king of Niué, I will end it with that of another. I wanted to bring back with me autograph letters from the native sovereigns for the wonderful collection of Her Majesty, the late Queen. Probably the last presents that she received from abroad were those that we brought back from the newest and most distant parts of the great empire. From the King of Tonga we brought a piece of red hand-woven cloth, which had been thrown about the shoulders of his ancestor by Captain Cook in 1772, and had been religiously preserved as an heirloom in the royal family out of reverence for the memory of the great "Tute"; from the King of Niué came the letter of which this is a translation:—

"Niué, 23 May, 1900.

"To Her Majesty

"Queen Victoria,

"Queen of Great Britain.

"Thanks to the Lord of Heaven, for through Him we have peace upon Earth. I, the King of Niué, send greeting to Your Majesty, the great Queen of Britain, and to your chiefs and governors. We, the King and Chiefs of Niué, send our thanks for the portrait of the Queen of Great Britain that has reached Niué. We, the chiefs and people of Niué, men, women, and children, gaze at the portrait.

"Thanks! Thanks! Great Thanks!

"Thanks for your great thought of us! Thanks for stretching out your arm to protect Niué-Fekai, Nukututaha (the land that stands alone), and Faka-hua-motu (the dependent).

"Tulou! Tulou! Tulou! (the form used in thanking a chief for help in war, implying a request for help in any future emergency).

"May the Lord of Heaven, of His grace, bless the treaty now made!

"That is all.

"I, Tongia,

"King of Niué-Fekai."

CHAPTER XI

TONGA REVISITED

OUR holidays were over; our real work was now to begin. As we steamed past the islet of Atatá and opened the low, monotonous shores of Tongatabu, stretching crescent-wise as far as the eye could reach, I wondered how the impulsive, faction-riven little people would receive me. Ten years ago I had been escorted to the steamer by the Lords and Commons in procession, but I had then been a Tongan Minister of the Crown working my hardest to bolster the independence of my adopted country; now I was an Englishman charged with a very different errand.

There is an apparent inconsistency about the two rôles that calls for explanation. Ten years bring many changes in the circumstances of little states. When I was last in Tonga, Hawaii was independent; three great Powers were still wrangling over Samoa; countless islands in the Pacific were yet unclaimed. All had fallen now, and eyes had been cast upon Tonga—the last independent state in the Pacific. She could make no resistance; her seizure was only a question of months, unless she had a powerful protector. For political, strategic, and geographical reasons England could not afford to tolerate a foreign Power in possession of the best harbour in the Pacific islands within striking distance of Fiji. And with the new agreement between England and Germany the last prop to Tongan independence had been cut away. Until then, the coaling station ceded to the Germans had been a guarantee against seizure by another Power, while British interests had acted as a check upon Germany. But now that the Germans had ceded all their treaty rights to us, we had either to take what was given to us, or leave the field open to others. In extending our protection, therefore, to the Tongans we were serving their interests even more than our own.

The reports which we had heard in Sydney, Fiji, and Samoa were very conflicting. All agreed in one thing—that, since the newspapers announcing us had been received, our arrival was awaited with anxiety; but, while some declared that the Tongans would resist the loss of their independence to the last man, others asserted that they would not be satisfied with a Protectorate, but would ask for annexation. I flattered myself that I knew the little people too well to believe the latter forecast.

As the white line of houses that marked the capital grew in definition, I began to notice changes. There stood the palace and its church as trim as ever within the stone-walled compound, but to the westward, where a native could be seen running up the British ensign, a wooden bungalow had replaced the picturesque old native-built consulate. These had been prosperous years with the Tongans; there was not a native-built house to be seen; trim little weather-board cottages had sprung up everywhere, and in the vacant space beside the government offices of my day there now stood a pretentious wooden building, the new House of Parliament. Naturally the traders, who had had the erecting of all these, had prospered too, and the line of stores on the eastern side of the town were resplendent in new paint. Two houses only in all the half-mile—ruinous, rain-washed, and neglected—told their own tale. They belonged to old Tungi and his son Tukuaho, my dear lamented colleague; with them and with their owners the years had dealt unkindly, as I shall presently relate.

The town was asleep in the sun; its trim, grassy streets stretching away inland were utterly deserted; it was like a toy town, fresh-painted from the shop before the miniature inhabitants have been taken out of their packing box. Nukualofa is, indeed, unlike any other town in the world. Not long ago a friend of mine encountered an American tourist, just landed from a steamer, gaping at a street corner where four ways meet, and asked him what he was looking at. "Sir," he replied, "they tell me that this is the business quarter of this capital, and I'm going to watch these four grass-walks till I see a human being. But I've wasted ten minutes, and I'll have to give it up."

We were boarded by my friend, Dr. Donald Maclennan, who, as the only practitioner in the group, is the hardest-worked man in Tonga. He has had a remarkable career. A Scotsman, educated in Canada, he practised first in San Francisco and afterwards in Hawaii, where he became a close friend of the native queen and the royalist party. When the Revolution of 1893 resulted in annexation by the United States, he made a tour round the Pacific islands without a definite intention of settling, and chanced to reach Tonga when the government was in desperate need of a medical officer. He accepted the post temporarily and has remained ever since, having by his skill, his independence, his distaste for politics, and his unselfish and fearless devotion to duty, inspired extraordinary confidence in the king, the people, and the Europeans—a feat which no foreigner has ever accomplished before.

It being necessary that we should take up our quarters on shore, we accepted Dr. Maclennan's hospitality with an alacrity that was almost indecent, since we knew, and he did not, the tax that we were to levy upon him. He had to submit to our society, to endless interruptions from messengers, and to an invasion by the entire court retinue on a memorable night when he was kept up till half-past two to witness the signing of the treaty in his dining-room. But he bore it all with untiring good humour to the end, and buried us beneath a load of obligation that would weigh very heavily upon me if he were conscious of it.

If any of us flattered himself that the town would wake up when it learned of our arrival, he was disappointed. Flags, it is true, fluttered up to the head of every staff, but the beach and the streets were still deserted. At three o'clock we ran the Tongan ensign to the masthead and saluted it, and the report of the first gun did certainly produce some stir. Little Tongan guardsmen began to bustle about the guard-room at the shore end of the wharf; presently a score of them hauled out a couple of five-pounders mounted on iron carriages, and trundled them to the foot of the flagstaff. The Tongan ensign fluttered down; the Jack was run up in its place and saluted with remarkable precision and regularity, for the guns must have been dangerously hot before the twenty-one had been fired. Presently a boat was manned, and a burly gentleman in frock-coat and silk hat, whom even at that distance I could recognise as Tui Belehake, embarked in her and came on board.

The lineal descendant of the gods had carried the ten years easily. His hair was a shade greyer, but the brightness of his eye and the natural gaiety of his laugh were not abated. With the exception of poor Tukuaho, all my old friends were well; they had heard of my coming through the newspapers, and rejoiced at it, though they knew not the cause (and here the hereditary laugh carried a tremor of nervousness); a princess had been born to the king six weeks before, and he, as His Majesty's father, chuckled at the thought of being a grandfather, and touched lightly on the still burning question of the king's marriage, which had not disturbed him, for all it had threatened revolution. And "Misa Beika" was back again. He laughed long and loud at this admission and the reminiscences that it evoked.

I must here digress to explain what had taken place since my term of office ten years before. In 1893 King George had died, at the age of ninety-seven, of a chill supposed to have been brought on by his obstinate habit of bathing at daybreak in the sea, and had been buried in a huge mound thrown up in the public square of Nukualofa, known as the Malaekula, or Red Square. Contrary to expectation, his great great-grandson, Taufa'ahau, had succeeded him without disturbance, under the title of George Tubou II. Not long after his accession he had dismissed Tukuaho, appointing him governor of Vavau, and had made Sateki, my auditor-general, premier in his stead. For a time the premier had had an European clerk, but the native government had gradually come to dispense with all Europeans except the Customs staff. This meant, of course, that it had sought unofficial and irresponsible advice from traders, and, during the last few months, the government was said to have been in the hands of a Hebrew firm, which contracted for the public supplies. In the eighth year of the king's reign it was felt that it was time for him to marry.

Overtures are said to have been made to more than one Polynesian princess, but public feeling ran high in favour of Ofa, a near kinswoman of Tukuaho, and therefore a chief woman of the Haatakalaua line. The betrothal was announced, and preparations had already been made for the royal wedding, when the king announced that he preferred Lavinia, Kubu's daughter, who, though descended from the Tui Tonga on her father's side, inherited inferior rank and congenital weakness from her mother. A meeting of all the high chiefs was summoned in Nukualofa, which recommended the king to make Ofa his queen; but His Majesty's reply, that, if he were not allowed to marry Lavinia, he would not marry at all, threw the meeting into confusion, and he was permitted to have his way under protest. It seems that the Lavinia party, though numerically inferior, trotted out that ancient stalking horse, the Constitution, to prove to their antagonists that inasmuch as "it shall not be lawful for any member of the royal family, who is likely to succeed to the throne, to marry any person without the consent of the king," the king was free to give consent to his own marriage with any person he pleased. This argument, so characteristic of the sophistry of the Tongan mind, was gravely set forth to me in a letter from my old colleague Asibeli Kubu, the father of His Majesty's preference; it reminded me of a legal judgment delivered during Mr. Baker's term of office, when two men, indicted for the theft of a pig, were sentenced to ten years' penal servitude for conspiracy, because in the evidence it had transpired that by mutual agreement one of the accused had kept watch while the other did the stealing. "Therefore," said his worship, "not only did you steal the pig, which is a small matter in itself, but you conspired together to steal it; and having sought in the index of this code for the clause concerning conspiracy, I find the minimum sentence to be ten years. To that term I sentence you, and you may think yourselves fortunate that I do not punish you for the theft as well."

To have the "Konisitutone" thrown at their heads was more than the nobles had reckoned upon. They might be wrong in law, but they knew what they wanted, and they broke up their meeting grumbling, and departed, each to his own home. The king, boycotted by all but his immediate adherents and the relations of his bride, kept close within the palace compound; the marriage feast was but sparsely attended, and the dissatisfaction of the people vented itself in attempts to burn public buildings and the houses of unpopular members of the royal party. The last of these incendiary attempts had occurred shortly before my visit.

Meanwhile, my old acquaintance Mr. Shirley Waldemar Baker, a person so remarkable in the Pacific that it will some day be a public duty to write his biography, had turned up again. Having spent several years in Auckland after his deportation by the High Commissioner, he had made overtures to the Free

Church of Tonga to accept him as their president. The Conference considered his application with the utmost gravity, and replied that, while they would be glad to welcome him as a minister, the office of president happened to be filled. That the Church of his own creation should treat him so was more than he could bear, and his next letter was a grim intimation that they would hear of him again. Those who knew him best may have felt an uncomfortable shiver at the threat, but none in his wildest dreams can have guessed how he would carry it out. For when Mr. Baker came back to Tonga it was as an emissary of the Church of England, speciously introduced to the Tongans as the *Jiaji a Vika* (the Church of Queen Victoria). Rebuffed by the Bishop of Honolulu, to whom the Bishop of London has delegated his authority over this part of the globe, he had persuaded the Bishop of Dunedin to give him a licence as lay reader. It is no part of my business to criticise this bishop's action, or to relate how the bishops of New Zealand intervened to dissuade him from going himself to Tonga to support his protégé, but I may be pardoned for asking under what authority of custom or ecclesiastical law one bishop can issue a licence for what is virtually the diocese of another.

The new Church was just the political weapon that the party of the rejected princess wanted. It offered a proof of discontent, it was a new experiment in Churches, and, above all, it annoyed the king. It was safer than burning houses, because, at the first whisper of reprisal, you could stand boldly forth and quote the Constitution about liberty of conscience. At the time of our visit Ofa had joined the new Church with most of her relations; and poor blind Tungi, her kinsman, had so far conquered his aversion to Mr. Baker as to permit services to be held in his premises. Mr. Baker had been careful not to define his exact position to the Tongans. All that a stole and surplus could do towards making him an ordained clergyman had been done. He did not bother the Tongans with any nonsense about Church government; the one thing he did understand was making a collection, and he held his first while I was at Nukualofa. Something under three hundred adherents subscribed nearly £200. I asked Ofa who kept the money. Had they churchwardens?

"Churchwardens," she said, "what are they?"

I explained. No, they had no churchwardens.

"Then who keeps the money?"

"Misa Beika."

It was melancholy to see how cruelly Fortune had used Tungi, whom I had left the most influential chief in Tonga. While his son Tukuaho was still alive his sight had begun to fail, and he had made the voyage to Samoa to consult a German oculist, who pronounced his case to be beyond hope. Hardly had night closed in upon him when Tukuaho, his only son and the most popular chief in Tonga, died suddenly of heart disease while riding with the king. Then came the jilting of Ofa, his near kinswoman, an insult to his family which must have hit him hard. He had retired to his little house in Nukualofa and was living quietly on the rents of the adjoining property, which he had enjoyed undisputed for many years, when the government suddenly put in a claim to it and dispossessed him, reducing him to poverty. I do not know the rights of the matter; I only know that the man who, failing royal issue, stood next to the throne, who was the most courtly and imposing of the chiefs of the old time, the last repository of ancient lore and tradition, was reduced to living in a hovel in which you would not stable a horse, blind, deserted, and in utter penury. A few weeks after our departure the last link with the past was severed by his death.

Beyond the birth of a princess three weeks before our arrival nothing had occurred to change the position. The king was in voluntary confinement in his compound, estranged from his chiefs, and consorting with three of his ministers, his kinsmen, and his guardboys, who tumbled into uniform only when a foreign ship was in port. The government of the country was nominally in the hands of old Sateki, my old auditor-general, then regarded as a sort of Sea-green Incorruptible, but now openly accused of acting at the behest of the firm of Hebrew merchants who were contractors to the government. The Treasury was empty and the salaries in arrear, but the country was not in debt, probably because its credit was not strong enough to carry a loan. The chronic depletion of the Treasury was due partly to the light-hearted Polynesian habit of turning money into goods on the first opportunity, and partly to the light-fingered ease with which the Treasury officials helped themselves to the contents of the till. It reminded me of old times to hear that a sum of £2,000 was missing from one of the sub-treasuries; that the treasurer, put upon his trial, had challenged an audit; and that the auditors, after completing their task, had stated that they were not quite sure whether the money had ever been received, or, if it had been received, whether it had been paid out legitimately or purloined. The foreshore was littered with dressed stone, intended for the thief-proof treasury which had been projected even in my time—"to keep out the rats," as the Chief Justice remarked facetiously, "only the rats that gnaw the money-bags will come in through the door." The Europeans made much of these defalcations as a factor in the general discontent, but in reality the grumbling was confined to the European traders, who naturally object to pay taxes under such conditions, for the Tongan does not greatly care what becomes of his money after he has paid it.

UILIAME TUNGI, THE BLIND CHIEF OF HAHAKE

CHAPTER XII

THE KING AND HIS MINISTERS

PUNCTUALLY at ten next morning we made our official landing, taking with us Her Majesty's presents to the King of Tonga—her portrait and a sword of honour inscribed with his name. The kodak representations of our procession were not flattering, but the large crowd of Tongans in the public square was too much preoccupied to perceive the humour in the show. For after passing the guard of honour on the wharf, we had to skirt the flagstaff, and we were told afterwards that, according to Mr. Baker, we should halt there and run up the Jack in place of the Geneva cross that fluttered aloft. But we passed the fatal spot, to the evident relief of the natives sitting on the grass and the disappointment of the Europeans who had their kodaks ready levelled.

The entire Tongan army was drawn up in the palace compound as a guard of honour, and its band played our national anthem very creditably as we approached. While the rank and file numbered about thirty, as in my time, I noticed that the roll of officers had increased until they formed a third line nearly as close as that of the men: their uniforms were so spotless and correct that some of my companions mistook them for Europeans. We were ushered into the throne-room, where two rows of chairs were drawn up facing one another, each with a becrowned armchair in the centre. On these, after the first greetings, we took our seats. I knew the room well, and it called up many memories, for here old King George had often received me informally, and all the state functions and receptions of foreign officials, which the old king disliked so heartily and underwent so cheerfully, had taken place. At an earlier date, when Mr. Baker had sought protection in the palace with his family, it had been Mrs. Baker's parlour, and from that epoch dated the fairy lights, wax flowers, and other incongruities. The faces of the king's suite were all familiar, for they had been my own colleagues when I was a Tongan like themselves. There was Fatafehi in his sober suit of black; Kubu, now swelled to the dignity of a sovereign's father-in-law, in a French-looking uniform with a cocked hat; Sateki, greyer and more care-lined than of old, and the two uniformed aides-de-camp, both famous cricketers in my day, but now inclining to obesity. Towering above all was the king, something over six feet in height and so broad in proportion that he cannot weigh much less than twenty stone. His tight uniform tunic, which enhanced his bulk, was covered with orders, which on closer examination proved to be the various classes of some Tongan decoration instituted by himself, designed by a jeweller in

Sydney, and not yet bestowed upon lesser men. He has a broad, intelligent, good-humoured face, with black, languid eyes, and a strong family likeness to his kinsman, poor Tukuaho. His manners are scarcely less genial and engaging, though he has not much taste for the society of Europeans, who cannot help feeling in his company *qu'il ne montre jamais le fond du sac*. Of his intelligence it is enough to say that, though he has never been abroad save for a few weeks spent in Auckland, he speaks English fairly well and reads the English newspapers; that he conducts his own correspondence with a typewriter, and can write Pitman's system of shorthand with facility. Though there are said to be flaws in his nature which prevent him from becoming a strong or popular ruler, he is by no means wanting in character. He has never been tempted by strong liquors, like so many of the Polynesian chiefs; his private life is regular; he has always known how to hold himself aloof from the lower sort of European; and I do not doubt that the insincerity of which he is so generally accused is really due to the desire of pleasing and the dislike of refusing a request. His health is not all that could be desired. Remembering the early death of all his family, until he alone was left to succeed his great-grandfather, we could not regard his stoutness, which had been characteristic of all of them, as a healthy sign, especially when we heard that he only took exercise in the palace compound at the direct order of his doctor. His mother and his uncles had all died of fatty degeneration of the heart when under forty, and none were so stout as he at twenty-seven.

A foreign language is apt to rust on the tongue after disuse for ten years, and my speech, presenting my credentials and the Queen's presents, ran less trippingly than I could have wished. But words came back to me as I talked, and, having plenty of time before me, I left politics alone. Then came the usual presentation of the naval officers, and a promise that the king would visit H.M.S. *Porpoise* on the morrow.

GEORGE TUBOU II., KING OF TONGA

Next morning we sent on shore for the royal standard of Tonga to hoist at the masthead when the king came on board. His Majesty came off in his barge, manned by a crew clad in black jumpers and *valas* fastened at the waist with a red sash, his band playing the Tongan national anthem as he left the wharf. Mounting the gangway alone, he seemed a little bewildered at finding a guard of honour drawn up to receive him, and not a little heated by the weight of his uniform and the orders that plastered it. His suite, consisting of Kubu, Fatafehi, and his aides-de-camp, quite filled the captain's cabin, and being the only medium of communication between hosts and guests, I found the burden of conversation rather difficult, for good manners in Tonga require that on formal occasions chiefs should confine themselves to monosyllables, and have their talking done for them. Once on deck, however, the ball rolled of itself, for the captain had rigged a mine, which the king fired with a button, sending a volcano of water into the air and slaying innumerable fish. The men then went through gun drill with the six-inch guns, which, it was explained, would carry with precision to the farthest limits of the island, and ended up with the imaginary ramming of an enemy. As the king left the side the three-pounders roared out a salute of twenty-one guns, perhaps the part of the entertainment which the king enjoyed best, for, whatever our mission might portend, it had so far left him the outward symbol of royalty.

That afternoon the draft treaty was sent to him, and then the tussle began. Besides the acknowledgment of a Protectorate, which would prevent the country falling into other hands, two definite concessions had to be made. In the port of Neiafu, in Vavau, Tonga possesses the best harbour in the Pacific —a land-locked basin with an easily defended entrance three or four miles long. In 1876, as the price of her treaty with Germany, Tonga had ceded a coaling-station in this harbour, and the Germans had dumped some twenty tons of coal upon their concession as a proof of occupation, and had thereafter forgotten all about it. Though we had succeeded to their treaty rights, it was necessary, not only to obtain the consent of the Tongans to the transfer, but to acquire the site for a fort to defend the coaling-station—a matter which had been neglected by the Germans. The second matter was more important. Tonga had made three treaties, ceding her jurisdiction over the subjects of the Powers concerned to their respective consuls, but, inasmuch as England only had a consular court in the group, it followed that Germans and Americans who committed a crime could not be punished for it, while the subjects of other Powers, in theory amenable to the native courts, in practice were free to break the law with impunity. The Samoa Convention gave the jurisdiction over Germans to us, but the experience of Zanzibar has taught us that a Protectorate without jurisdiction over all foreigners is a very unsatisfactory arrangement. The only person who could legally confer the jurisdiction over foreigners upon our courts was the King of Tonga, who nominally possessed it, and this he had to be asked to do. If he had been anxious to part with his responsibilities there would have been little difficulty, but Tongans share with schoolboys a light-hearted contempt for the dangers of responsibility, and are, besides, rather proud of their law courts. We soon found that it was to be a long and tortuous business, calling for all the patience that we had at command.

It was common gossip that the most influential chiefs and a large number of the people were secretly in favour of a Protectorate, but that the real obstacle was the king. Not long before my visit he had received a letter from the deposed queen of Hawaii, greeting him as the last independent sovereign of the Polynesian race, and condoling with him upon the threatened loss of his independence. Fully alive to the advantages it would give him in securing him from the constant demands for compensation pressed upon him by foreigners, he feared that if he voluntarily ceded a Protectorate his opponents would accuse him of having sold his country; and he thought, no doubt, that it was the first step towards depriving him of the outward pomp of royalty which was so dear to him. One cannot but understand his attitude, though it was inconsistent with the welfare of his country.

At my first private interview with the king as in duty bound I asked to be presented to the queen and the new-born princess. The queen was still confined to her room. His Majesty led me upstairs. The whole of the wall space on the staircase is filled by a colossal equestrian portrait of the first Kaiser, very ill-painted, and so large that the frame must either have been carried in piecemeal or the palace built round it. It belonged to the period when the Germans acquired their coaling-station and Mr. Baker was decorated with the Red Eagle of Prussia. There are four large rooms on the upper floor, three of them furnished in European style, and the fourth used as a lumber-room for the toys and litter which Polynesian chiefs buy so readily and tire of so quickly. We found Her Majesty in the best bedroom, which is furnished with a four-post bed and Brussels carpet. Everything was immaculately clean, and there was nothing to show that the room did not belong to an European lady. The queen wore a pink silk wrapper, and was sitting in a low chair with her brown baby on her knee. Her illness, which at one time had caused great anxiety, accounted for her pallor and her delicate appearance. Though she is not handsome, her slenderness and her delicacy of feature give her a certain air of distinction, and, like all Tongan women of good family, she has pretty manners. Having made my christening present and kissed the baby, I took my leave. During the queen's illness Dr. Maclennan had a busy time, for, though the king has an implicit belief in European treatment, the old ladies about the court insist upon administering nostrums of their own on the principle of "more medicine, quicker cure." It is only by simulated outbursts of indignation that Dr. Maclennan can get his orders obeyed.

In surgery alone do the Tongans frankly admit their helplessness. An old shed in our host's compound had been hastily converted into an operating-room, in order that the presence of a naval surgeon to assist in operations might be turned to account. For several days in succession the two doctors were operating on bad cases of elephantiasis, the relations of the patients camping outside to act as hospital nurses. Even under these unfavourable conditions the patients all made rapid recovery, but there was one painful case in which the patient deliberately preferred death. A young man, while pig-shooting in the bush, had put a charge of shot into his own leg, shattering the ankle. There was nothing for him but amputation, but when his relations heard that he must lose his foot, they refused to allow the operation. They would try herbs, they said, and for a day or two they brought reports that he was better. Gangrene at last set in, and while there was yet time I went to reason with the lad's mother.

Secretly, I fear, the reflection that if he lived the lad would be a helpless cripple on their hands had some weight with them. At last they were brought so far as to put him on a litter to carry him to the operating-room, but their hearts failed them in the end and he never came. The lad himself seemed to prefer death, so great is the Polynesian's horror of mutilation.

It is not always for human beings that Dr. Maclennan is asked to prescribe. Having been much troubled by his neighbours' pigs, he gave public warning of his intention of shooting intruders at sight. The very next night he executed his threat by moonlight, and heard the trespasser make off with an agonised squeal. Next morning he received an urgent summons from the inspector of police, a particular friend of his, to see his favourite pig which had been taken violently ill. One glance was enough to show him what ailed it, and he said, "The pig is very ill; it cannot live many hours, but if you kill and eat it at once, the meat will be perfectly wholesome." The owner took his advice, but unhappily, in carving the meat, he came across a bullet. It cost the doctor more than the value of the pig to patch the friendship up. By dint of a happy mingling of kindliness and mock ferocity he contrives to get his orders obeyed, and the people have an extraordinary respect and affection for him.

I had more than one interview with the chief justice—not the somnolent old gentleman of ten years ago, but William Maealiuaki, who was then but an over-intelligent Radical member of Parliament. Persecution (he was an exile for conscience' sake in Mr. Baker's time), prosperity, or promotion had not been good for him; he had parted with even that little meed of modesty which adorns even the loftiest eminence. He took his duties very seriously, however, and whenever he came to see me it was to resolve some legal doubt that had arisen in the course of his duties on the bench. "You see," he said one day, "I have to be more careful now that there are *loya* listening to my judgments."

"Lawyers?" I inquired in surprise.

"Yes," he said, with pride; "and that is your work."

It was, I confess with shame, only too true. In Mr. Baker's days no one knew the law—not even the magistrates—and, as judgments went by favour, a suitor lost nothing by pleading his own case. But the code which I had drafted for them changed all that. It was furnished with an index, and a copy could be bought for less than a dollar. As soon as it transpired that there was nothing in it to preclude one Tongan from pleading for another, every native who could talk better than he could work took to loafing about the police courts, offering himself as a mouthpiece to the litigants. His fees were tentative at first—"give me what you like if I get you off," and so on—but now he likes to be paid in advance, though you can brief him with a sucking-pig and keep him going with an armful of yams as a "refresher." The *loya* who enjoyed the largest practice were those who had the code at their finger-ends, and had acquired a high reputation for obscuring the issue and confusing the common sense of the court.

A TONGAN GIRL

The chief justice also gave me a summary of the birth and death returns for the nine years ending December, 1899. I do not regard them with any confidence, partly because I know the haphazard way in which the registers are kept, and partly because, assuming the total population of the kingdom to be not less than 19,000,[10] the death-rate is represented as low as eleven per thousand and the birth-rate as high as twenty-six per thousand, which is very unlikely, seeing that families of more than three living children are rare. Nevertheless, the Tongans are all agreed that, in spite of a devastating epidemic of measles in 1893, there has been an increase of population of over 200 in the nine years; the returns say 203. I think myself that the population is stationary, or slightly decreasing, but that there has been no very marked decline, as in Hawaii, New Zealand, and Fiji since the beginning of the nineteenth century. The people, moreover, are so fearful of foreign epidemics and so sensitive about quarantine that there is not much likelihood of a sudden decline for many years to come.

It was very pleasant to renew acquaintance with the European colony at the Consulate. Many of them are prosperous merchants, and their appearance of rude health justified the saying that the climate of Tonga is the healthiest in the Pacific. The little gathering did not pass off without incident. While I was talking to two new arrivals an elderly and rather feeble little gentleman in black entered the room, and my two visitors hastily seized their hats and took their leave before I had had time to exchange a word with them. The features of my new visitor seemed familiar, but the suspicion that crossed my mind while he was talking affably of the weather and the earthquake and other general topics died away, as I noticed how decrepit and broken he seemed. Suddenly through the open window I saw a party of new arrivals stop short, hesitate for a moment, and then turn tail, and knowing that there was but one man in all Tonga who could produce this effect, I recognised my visitor. It was Mr. Shirley Waldemar Baker himself. He was greatly changed from the masterful and prosperous minister of King George, whose name had been a byword throughout the Pacific and Australasia. His gains were all gone; years of hard living had played havoc with his health and prematurely aged him; he seemed to have lost even the self-confidence behind which he had concealed his lack of education. And yet even in this broken state he was able to make himself feared. Why he came and what he wanted I do not know; his motive can scarcely have been friendly after the criticism of his proceedings that I had been obliged to publish ten years before. Probably he wished to prove to the adherents of his new Church that he was on terms with the authorities.

CHAPTER XIII

VAVAU

I NEED not detail all the moves in a game of hide-and-seek played in a South Sea capital with private agents for pieces. It lasted a full six weeks, and like other hard-fought games, it is pleasanter in the retrospect than it was in the playing. There were pauses in the game, and in one of these I steamed off to Vavau, carrying with me Fatafehi, His Majesty's father, to choose the fort and the coaling-station.

Fatafehi, Tui Belehake—"Two-belly," as the blue-jackets irreverently called him—is a lineal descendant of the gods, and too exalted a personage to sit upon an earthly throne. So while his son, inheriting through his mother Fujipala, the late king's granddaughter, wears the crown (fashioned by a Sydney jeweller out of a metal that was charged for as gold, but apt to develop verdigris in damp weather), he is content to discharge the humbler office of Minister of Lands combined with that of Speaker of the Parliament. To assist in determining the boundaries of the coaling-station, he brought with him a body-servant and a young man armed with a theodolite, an instrument which proved of great value to us, though not in the way intended by its makers. By his charming manners and his hearty laugh he endeared himself to all on board, though he could not speak a word of any language but his own, and I was not always at hand to interpret. He lived nominally in the captain's cabin, but though he ate heartily and was quite at his ease, he showed the instinct of an old sailor in carrying up his blanket to the deck, where he was found in the morning asleep in a canvas chair.

Having a curiosity to visit Falcon Island, we did not take the direct route to Vavau. Early in 1896 Falcon Reef, then a patch of coral awash at low water, suddenly broke into eruption and cast up an island of pumice stone more than 100 feet high. Mr. Shirley Baker, who watched the eruption from a schooner, described it to me as a terrific spectacle, as indeed it must have been, for the sea had access to the crater, and was flung aloft in explosions of steam. As soon as the mass was cool enough to stand upon, the Tongan ensign was hoisted upon it, and the new island became a portion of King George's dominions. It did not swell his revenues, for, when I passed it four years later, it had shrunk to less than half its original size, and every roller that broke upon its shores brought down a landslip of pumice which covered the surface of the sea for some distance. H.M.S. *Porpoise* had examined it in 1899, and had reported it as a reef barely awash, and her officers were anxious to see whether there had been any change since their last visit. We sighted it at three o'clock in the afternoon. The sea was breaking heavily, and as we drew near we were astonished to find a black hump protruding nine feet above the waves. It was impossible to make a closer examination in the boats, but the navigating lieutenant was satisfied that the restless island was emerging again from the sea.

Early next morning we steamed into Neiafu Harbour. Something unusual about the vegetation on the outer island had struck us as we came in, but we were not prepared for the scene of desolation that met us as we swung round Utulei Point to the anchorage. The centre of a terrific cyclone had struck the island on April 2nd, 1900, just a week before our arrival. Scarce a house was left standing; the trees were naked; the graceful palms were mere ragged broomsticks stuck aslant in the earth. In the steamy calm the water of the harbour was like oil, and it was impossible to picture the wild fury that had beset the place but seven days past. We landed, half deafened by the reverberating echo of the saluting guns, to pay our official visit to George Finau, now promoted to be governor over the people whose hereditary lord he is. Abnormally thick-set when I knew him, he was now elephantine in girth, and if his twelve-year-old son maintains his present rate of growth, his little finger will be thicker than his father's loins.

The formal reception being over, we were free to stroll through the town. The ruin was complete; the government offices were an untidy heap of lumber; the great native church, the last work of King George of pious memory, had collapsed; its mighty roof, unshipped from the supporting posts, but still held together by its sinnet lashings, lay careened like a stranded hull—the pulpit was overturned, the flooring ripped from end to end. Never again, the king told me, would such a house be built again, for the degenerates of these days prefer corrugated iron. Already the Roman Catholics were pointing to their concrete church, still standing like an island among the general wreckage, as a proof of Divine warranty, a little tempered perhaps by reason of a gaping rent in the tower. The people were living in the open air, crawling into the cover of their ruined houses to shelter from the rain. Poor souls! they bore their misfortunes with a light heart, though the crop of orange trees, from which they get their living, were uprooted, and the cocoanuts would not recover for two years. Every boat in the island was busy bringing food from the less stricken villages, and the men were saving something from the wreck by turning the fallen cocoanuts into copra.

Next day we set forth in the ship's boats to survey the German coaling-station in the bight of the harbour. The shore is here a coral reef, upheaved about fifteen feet above the sea. The soil is shallow, but, like all limestone formations, very productive, and covered with plantations and cocoanut trees.

On the further side was the open sea, for this part of the harbour is a mere breakwater, tapering away to a boat passage in the bight of the harbour, where the land is only two furlongs across. The Germans had done themselves handsomely, and had allowed no concern for the welfare of the natives to interfere with their wishes. Starting from the boat passage, they had annexed a generous strip of country for a distance of half a mile, regardless of the fact that many families, who had never been consulted, were robbed of all their planting land at a stroke of the pen. These families had continued placidly to cultivate their plantations, and they were now sitting silent in the road to hear their fate. The coal, the sole evidence of their dilemma, was now a hillock of crumbling, chocolate-coloured gravel, overgrown with creepers and long unrecognisable as fuel.

THE CHURCH BUILT BY KING GEORGE I.

Wrecked by the cyclone

THE GOVERNMENT OFFICES AT VAVAU

Wrecked by the cyclone. A female convict is clearing away the wreckage

We chained the boundary with a sounding-line, the owners cheerfully pointing it out without any attempt to diminish the area, which proved to contain no less than thirty acres of good planting land. This being far more than we wanted, I saw an opportunity for securing a site for the fort as well. Calling them together in an open place, I announced that though England had succeeded to all the German concession, yet she would restore to them six-sevenths of this good land, and in return would only ask for a little plot of bad land in another part of the harbour. Then we chained out a rectangular piece, with a frontage of 200 yards, 100 yards deep on one side and 140 at the other, and the natives showed their delight by clearing the boundary and planting lines of cocoanuts to mark it. The ship's carpenter made huge broad arrows in cement at the corners on the sea face, and erected blocks of stone, similarly marked, at the inner corners.

Meanwhile the navigating officer was taking angles with a sextant on the sea front, and Unga, Fatafehi's secretary, was following him about with his theodolite like a faithful dog. So pathetic was his anxiety that his ancient instrument should be put to use that the lieutenant at last took pity on him, and set it up. The first glance showed him that the metal cap had rusted to the lens, and when he wrenched it off a cry of agony was wrung from Unga, as who should say, "Now you've done it!" For years he had been pretending to survey the boundaries in land disputes with the cap on, and the erection of the instrument had always sufficed to settle the dispute, and here was an Englishman, albeit possessing the occult knowledge of a naval lieutenant, ruthlessly destroying the *mana* of his weapon for ever. But when he was shown that he could look through the telescope, which had formerly only presented darkness to his eye, and his instructor even promised to give him lessons in the science of angles, his delight knew no bounds. For days afterwards the lieutenant and his disciple were familiar spectacles in the chart- room, and the former, who came to be a little bored with his pupil's ardour, admitted that he had shown amazing aptitude, and that he could take rough angles and calculate area with approximate accuracy.

It was not easy to select the site for the protecting fort owing to the wealth of choice, but eventually we found what we wanted. Fatafehi undertook to "square" the owner, the descendant of a Portuguese deserter from a ship, who had found favour with the Finau Ulukalala of Mariner's time. So far from receiving the idea of a British fort on Tongan territory with coolness, the Tongans seemed to be pleased with it, especially when I hinted that the garrison might consist of Tongans under the command of a British officer. They are a race of warriors, condemned for the present to live upon the traditions of their ancestors' exploits, and soldiering is to them the most noble of occupations; indeed, no commander could ask for more promising material for troops, for alone among South Sea races they had evolved the idea of discipline, and preferred to capture entrenched positions by direct assault.

The remainder of our visit was given to sight-seeing. I was anxious to revisit the Hunga cave, twice-famed by Mariner and Byron. In 1890 a westerly swell had prevented me from diving into it, but this time Finau had promised to provide guides from the best divers in the island, and to put no obstacles in my way if the weather made the adventure possible. But to my disappointment a westerly swell again set in, and the guides backed his declaration by refusing to risk their own skins. I had to admit to myself that it would have been a poor ending to my trip to be sent home in bandages, after defying the advice of the guides, especially as I had been warned by Mr. H. J. Marshall, r.n., who was a midshipman on H.M.S. *Calliope* when Captain Aylen explored the cave in 1852, that the feat was difficult even in calm weather. Captain Sir J. Everard Home being anxious to have the cave explored in order to test William Mariner's story, selected Mr. J. F. R. Aylen, then a Master's Assistant, now a Post-Captain retired, as being the best diver in the ship. He was taken to the indicated position of the cave's mouth in the galley, and furnished with a lead line and two natives as guides. There was no sea on, but the dive is a long one—one fathom down and five fathoms along the passage before it is possible to rise into the cave. Aylen was, I believe, the first white man to enter the cave since Mariner, and, being something of a draughtsman, he made a sketch of the interior, which was afterwards turned into a picture by an artist in Sydney. The return dive was not so successful. The great difficulty in diving out of these submarine caves is that, your face being downwards, you are deceived by the reflected light into coming up too soon. Captain Aylen scratched his back so severely with the stalactites that the wounds did not heal for two months.

With Finau for guide we rode out to see the famous fortress of Feletoa, at whose ramparts the most stirring of Mariner's adventures[11]were enacted. Those who have read this classic in the literature of travel will remember that when Toeumu revolted against her nephew, Finau Ulukalala, in 1810, the entire population of the island was entrenched at Feletoa in the largest and strongest fortress ever built in Tonga. Finau besieged the place with an army of 5,000 men and artillery taken from the captured ship *Port-au-Prince*, but, after an ineffective siege of many months, was obliged to make terms with the enemy. The place lies four miles from Neiafu, on a deep bay communicating with the same harbour. Descending from the modern village which lies just outside the landward defences, we came upon the outer rampart at a spot about two furlongs from the beach and 100 feet above it. We traced the triple line of ditches and earthworks for 200 yards, to a spot near the angle, where they made a semicircular sweep to enclose a fissure in the earth before trending inland. This rift was the secret of the long resistance to Finau's army. The story runs that, a few years before the siege, a man weeding yams in the gardens above noticed that his dog disappeared and returned with a dripping coat. Fresh water is too rare in Vavau for this to be allowed to pass, and the next day the dog was followed. He vanished into a hole in the coral rock, and after several minutes, returned dripping as before.

Torches were procured and a man scrambled down. The passage gradually widened until, at a depth of forty or fifty feet, it became a large cave full of water of unknown depth. It was this discovery that led to the choice of Feletoa as the site for the fortress that was to contain the entire population of the island. We explored the cave, and found that the water was clear, but slightly brackish. Probably it rises and falls with the tide, and the whole island, like Niué, contains similar reservoirs of fresh water beneath its crust. Mariner says that Finau had the ramparts levelled with the ground, but, to judge by the works still remaining, his commands must have been but grudgingly obeyed, for it would not take much to put the place into a state of defence again.

From a photograph by   *J. Martin,*
Auckland.

THE LAND-LOCKED HARBOUR OF VAVAU

On the right is the flat-topped hill of Talau; in the distance Hunga Island and Mariner's Cave; the entrance stretches away beyond it

Surveying the fort, even in its dismantled and overgrown condition, we could well believe that it had a most imposing appearance. The land-locked inlet, with its vista of hazy islands to seaward and its brilliant reflections, broken here and there by light puffs of wind, must have been a fit setting for the lofty triple rampart alive with warriors in their war-harness. Of their Homeric deeds in the great siege you may read in the pages of Dr. Martin, who, if he wrote no epic, contrived at least to lose nothing of the romance in William Mariner's story.

CHAPTER XIV

BETWEEN THE ACTS

O N our return to Nukualofa, we found that the hurricane had had its bearing upon the negotiations. The king had promised to assemble all his chiefs, and of the vessels at his disposal one had come to grief and the remaining two were engaged in the pressing work of carrying food for the relief of the homeless and hungry people of Vavau. There was reason in his demand that he should not be asked to take the sole responsibility of signing a momentous treaty, an act which might afterwards be used against him by any disaffected chief, and there was nothing left to do but to urge more rapid action and sit still until the chiefs came. While my native agents were employed in allaying the wild rumours that had been set abroad among the people, we were free to do some sight-seeing.

We made an expedition to Bea to inspect the English guns, said to be those abandoned by the landing party from H.M.S. *Favourite*, which came to grief at the siege of Bea in 1840, and often cited by the Tongans as evidence of how they beat a British man-o'-war. We found two of them half buried in the grass in the middle of the village, and a third serving as a fencing-post. They all bore the same mark:— that is, 9-pounders, cast in Portsmouth in 1813, and weighing 8 cwt. 3 qrs. 14 lbs. It seemed unlikely that frigates in 1840 would have been carrying iron guns cast in 1813, but an old man who had taken part in the defence of Bea and old Tungi cleared up the difficulty between them. The relics of the *Favourite* had all been removed by another ship, sent expressly from Sydney in the following year, and these guns had been bought from the captain of a whaler which was wrecked at the eastern part of the island some years after the siege. For many years whalers and trading vessels had carried guns like these, which they had probably bought cheap from the Admiralty, for purposes of trade.

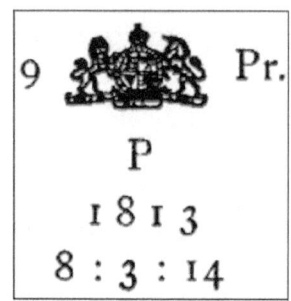

One of our excursions was to the colony of flying-foxes at Hihifo, where I wished to renew my acquaintance with old Ata, the hereditary lord of the western district, who had not been on cordial terms with the king since the royal marriage. His village lies upon the shores of Maria Bay, so named by Tasman when he discovered the island in 1643, and it is close to Kanakubolu, where the temporal kings were always crowned, and from which they take their title of Tui Kanakubolu. The ancient tree under which they sat was overthrown (*absit omen*) in a gale a few years ago, and the present king caused pieces of the wood to be inlaid in the throne of the royal chapel. But the feature of the place is the flying-fox colony. Four or five great *toa* trees stand in the village square, and many thousands of these great fruit-eating bats roost there in the sunshine, hanging head downward like noisome fruit, crawling, scratching, quarrelling, killing the foliage with their droppings and poisoning the air with their reek. At nightfall they set forth in long procession for the banana plantations, levying toll on them as far as Mua, fifteen miles distant, and returning to their perch before daybreak. In no sense are they sacred, and away from the colony they may be shot, but it is inauspicious to shoot them in the village itself, because then they would go away and dire misfortune would happen. For every great family in Tonga has its death portent; with the Fatafehi it is the splitting of a great banyan tree; with the Tui Kanakubolu it is the roar of breakers on the reef in calm weather; with the Ata it is the sudden migration of the flying-foxes from the trees in Kolovai.

We had a delightful ride along the grassy road shaded with orange trees ripening to harvest. On either side of the road lay wide tracts of uncultivated bush, and I was sorry to see, mingled with the matted foliage, the ill-omened pink flowers of the *Talatala hina*. In the Parliament of 1891, when I sat on the Treasury bench, a panic bill had been hurried through, making it penal for any landowner to have this plant on his land after March, 1902. If the fines then provided were to be enforced now, the government would require no other source of revenue, for the plant, then confined to a small district at the back of the island, has now advanced to within a few miles of Nukualofa. It is a tough, creeping vine, armed with sharp, reflexed thorns, deep-rooted and very difficult to eradicate. Throwing its wicked arms about a young tree it thrusts them up to the light, choking its support in its tangled embrace. The story that it was introduced by a trader in the straw of a packing-case is, perhaps, mythical, but it was certainly unknown in Tonga thirty years ago. Unless strong measures are taken to check it, there will come a day when neither cocoanuts nor yams can be planted any more. Then Tonga, overrun with a tangle of thorny vines, swarming with hornets, will not be a pleasant place to live in.

This plant is not the only pest for which packing-straw is said to be accountable. Between 1890 and last year hornets were introduced. They have multiplied so rapidly that it is now unsafe to brush through the thick undergrowth in which they build their nests. We had lived on shore in Nukualofa for three weeks before we saw any, but on a never-to-be-forgotten day in May, they made up for their neglect. About ten the air began to vibrate with an angry hum, and we noticed a few hornets cruising about the eaves of the verandah. An hour later they were knocking against the window panes and crawling about the walls, seeking entrance to the house. At lunch-time the dining-room was full of them, and their angry hum almost drowned conversation. They were making for the darker places, the shade of the shuttered bedrooms, the backs of pictures and the folds of curtains. They took no notice of us, but every now and then a couple would meet in the upper air, fall pat upon the floor, and take to crawling. As there seemed no reason why they should not choose to fall between the collar and the neck, or crawl up the legs, we thought it time to seek sanctuary. But there was none. Every corner of the house was theirs, and in the pitiless sun outside the air was black with them. A hot argument arose about this phenomenon, some of us maintaining that they were swarming, and, like bees, would gather about their queen; others, who knew them better, that they were male and female, and that this was their pairing time. To that emotional hour I owe all my learning about hornets. The brute so heavily barred with black stripes that he looks a wicked brown, is the male, who has no sting, and may be trodden on with impunity; the bright yellow beasts are females, with a barbed sting nearly as long as their bodies. We disturbed the economy of Nature that day. Our host had a five-gallon jar of some American insect powder, and we lighted censers of the acrid stuff in every room until we had to dash into the air to breathe. Would that I could remember the name of that powder, to give its inventor a gratuitous advertisement! In half an hour our enemies were all upon the floor at the mercy of a soft broom and a dust-pan. We filled two buckets with their kicking bodies, and fed the kitchen fire with them. We heard next day that every house in Nukualofa, from the king's palace to the pigsties, had been made uninhabitable, but that at sunset they had disappeared, to be seen no more till next year.

Our escort of policemen were most obliging fellows. One was a Wesleyan, the other a Free Churchman, and the friendly theological discussions in which they indulged from time to time showed that the bitter sectarian hatred, so sedulously nurtured by Mr. Baker, had quite died away. Ten years before a Wesleyan could not have hoped for the humblest government appointment.

I was bursting with the showman's pride as we rode into Kolovai, having wrought the expectations of my companions to the highest pitch. I begged them not to look up until we halted under the trees. When I gave the word they looked up, and then they looked at me. Surely these were not the trees! But the state of the foliage left no doubt upon that point. We called an old woman out of a neighbouring house, and there was no mistaking the concern in her tone as she was telling her tale. Four days before, she said, at an hour before sunset, an albino flying-fox had circled over the village, settling at last on the branches of a tree over against the door of Ata's house. Early in the morning it had flown over the trees, and the entire colony, which was just settling down to sleep after its nocturnal excursion in search of food, took to wing and followed it. Not a flying-fox had visited the town since.

Our escort were very grave over the news. "You know our belief," said Salesi; "when the *beka* flies away, it is a sign to Ata's family. Twice have I known it so; the last time when Ata's son, who was a tutor in the Wesleyan college, died without warning, and it was always so in the time of our fathers." I found old Ata and his wife in excellent health and spirits to all outward seeming, though naturally the flying-foxes were not mentioned in our conversation. Next day Nukualofa was buzzing with the news of Ata's approaching dissolution. Ridicule of the superstition was always met with the remark, "Well, wait and see; it may not be this week, or this month, but none the less Ata has not long to live"—a statement which, as the old gentleman's age verged upon seventy, we were not in a position to gainsay. The king, who is as enlightened as anyone in his kingdom, was scarcely less positive. "It is one of those things," he said, "that one would fain laugh at, but it has come true so often that one is compelled, against his will, to believe it true." Well, ten days passed, and Ata attended the great council of chiefs assembled to consider the treaty, the halest and liveliest of the old gentlemen present. I noticed that while he was chaffing two members of the cabinet, the bystanders regarded him with the tender, melancholy interest which is supposed to be bestowed upon the man in the condemned cell, and this may have told upon his spirits; for certain it is that a few weeks after my departure from the islands I received the news that he was dead. That superstition will die hard, and if I were Ata's successor I would see to it that a few of the flying-foxes were caught and tied to their perches by a string.

From a photograph by *J. Martin,*
Auckland.

THE COLONY OF FLYING FOXES AT KOLOVAI

They were seen on the same trees by Vason, the renegade missionary, in 1799

One morning two of Kubu's nieces, accompanied by an aged duenna, brought presents from their uncle, who perhaps felt that, since his dual rôle as my friend and the king's father-in-law had been beyond his powers, some pledge of our old intimacy would not be out of place. Among the things was a set of stamps for printing the native cloth, and when I hastened to appropriate these, the younger sister, who has kittenish manners, broke in with "Oh, but *I* made these; they are not for you, they are for this gentleman!" Webber did his best to rise to this embryonic flirtation, but it died stillborn in nods and smiles for want of an interpreter. As the conversation dragged and the ladies showed no consciousness of having discharged their mission, it was suggested that they should face the camera by way of complimentary dismissal. They were nothing loath, but the elder sister stipulated for the loan of a silk handkerchief to hide her neck. As she had the ordinary English neck of not ungraceful outline, and her sister, who had no neck to speak of, showed none of this bashfulness, our curiosity was aroused. It was thus that we discovered the Tongan ideal of female loveliness. The perfect woman must be fat—that is most imperative— her neck must be short (like the younger sister's); she must have no waist, and if Nature has cursed her with that defect she must disguise it with draperies, or submit to be "miscalled" in the streets of Nukualofa; her bust and hips and thighs must be colossal. The woman who possesses all these perfections will be esteemed chief-like and elegant, and her nose will not matter, though, if she have that organ flat to the face, she will be painting the lily. There chanced to be an illustrated paper on the table, and when we showed them the wasp-waisted ladies in the fashion plates they chuckled with amusement and derision. The king, whom I afterwards asked for a definition of female beauty, confirmed all they said, and added a philosophical explanation of his own. He said that the human eye demanded a sufficiency in the things presented to it; if they were insufficient, it found them ugly. The Tongan dress did not conceal the form as does the European; consequently Tongan ladies were expected to be satisfying in respect of the portions of their anatomy that are exposed to view. We may be content with a simpler explanation. In days gone by the chief women got more to eat than their inferiors, and *embonpoint* became a chiefly attribute. This mark of high birth being once stereotyped, men chose their wives accordingly, and the Tongan dames will grow stouter with every generation. It is not a pleasing prospect.

At one stage in our negotiations the king began to develop a remarkable capacity for digression. At any other time his excursions would have been interesting, for, untrained as he is, he possesses the historical and literary instinct, and he can tell a good story. I think that it was while we were discussing the relative merits of the Tongan synonyms for the word Protectorate that he suddenly inquired my opinion upon the close connection between the Tongan and Hebrew tongues. I hastened to turn the subject, assuring him that I had never thought about the matter, for that hoary folly of the Ten Lost Tribes was in the air; but he said that it was his own discovery. Someone had given him a Hebrew book to look at, and in one page he had found no less than six Tongan words. He quoted the conjunction *kaeuma'a*, which, he said, occurred in both languages with the same meaning. On another occasion he brought out the piece of hand-made red cloth which I was to take home as a present to the Queen. This had been given by Captain Cook to the Tamahá, the noblest lady in the land, and had been preserved by the family of the Tui Haatéiho. It was a large piece of hand-made woollen cloth, rather loosely woven and of a rusty red colour, with a black selvedge edge, and it smelt strongly of sandalwood oil, having been worn on great occasions by chiefs anointed with that precious essence. It is now, I believe, among the curiosities in the royal collection at Windsor Castle. He then told me some native traditions of Cook's visit. When the vessels were seen approaching Hihifo in 1773 there was a heated discussion among the Tongans as to whence they came. The king mimicked the querulous intonation of the old Tongans very funnily. "Whence come they?" said one. "Seuke!" exclaimed the old chief, Eikinaba, a noted wit in his day, "why, from the land of riches— from Babalangi!" (or, as we might say, from Brobdignag), and the nickname Babalangi has stuck to Europeans ever since. *Ba-ki-langi* ("shooting up to heaven") is the derivation which Fatafehi favours, meaning that the ships' masts reached to the sky. When the Tongans boarded the *Resolution*, the same chief, Eikinaba, noticed a strange yam on the deck and picked it up. "I *give* you that," said Tute (Cook), and from that day this kind of yam was called the *Kivi*. Favoured perhaps by the cooler climate and the new soil, this yam has grown to colossal dimensions. Cook had probably brought it from Rarotonga, or from Tahiti.

Of the number of curious petitions to which I had to listen, the strangest came from a singularly ill-favoured private in the king's guards. He waylaid me in the road with a letter in an official envelope, which I took to be a message from the palace. It contained, however, a long and confused recital of the love troubles of one Josefa, who, being enamoured of Ana, the daughter of an Englishman and the most beautiful *taahine* in all the world, had eloped with her into the bush. At this, as it appeared, Ana's father, the Englishman, had been much incensed (as was not unnatural), and had haled Josefa before the British Consul, who had fulminated threats, scaring Josefa out of his wits. Would I therefore order the Consul to marry the pair out of hand, for, loving each other with so consuming a passion, how were they to wait five years?

When I asked who had written this mysterious letter in the envelope superscribed "On His Tongan Majesty's Service," the bearer's sheepish look betrayed the fact that he had written it himself. In fact, he himself was Josefa, and, looking at his countenance, I could only wonder at the lady's taste. It then transpired that she was barely sixteen (love's arrows strike early in these latitudes), and he had been guilty of nothing less than the abduction of a British subject under age, for her father was an English carpenter legally married to a Tongan wife. I could only counsel the love-sick guardsman to win consent from the father, or in the alternative to contain his soul in patience till she was twenty-one. It seemed to be cold comfort, for the father had terminated their last interview by chasing him with a carpenter's adze, and I suspect that by this time the friendly forest has again swallowed up the pair, and the carpenter is abroad with his chopper.

The eaves-dropping nuisance at the palace was little less tiresome than it had been ten years before, when one had to bawl state secrets into the deaf ears of old King George. One morning, while I was explaining the treaty to the king's ministers, I chanced to see in a mirror the reflection of a girl on her hands and knees, with eyes and ears wide open at a chink of the door, which she had pushed ajar. Our eyes met in the glass, and she scurried away like a frightened rabbit, but I was not surprised to hear afterwards that many of my remarks were being quoted verbatim in the town. Accordingly when the king asked me one morning to come into his private chapel to hear an important communication, I understood his reasons. As we crossed the compound he remarked in a loud voice for the benefit of the sentry, "Yes, all that remains of the sacred tree has been inlaid in the state chair like your coronation stone in England. Come and see." Sitting on the two thrones on the daïs we were at last secure from eaves-droppers, and could talk freely. He told me that there were two Tongan words that expressed the feeling of his country towards England— *falala* and *faha'a*. Rising and leaning against one of the pillars of the aisle, he said, "This is *faha'a*: then I spring away from it so, and cry, 'Oh! but it won't bear my weight!' and you say, 'Don't be afraid; *falala be ki ai*' ('Lean upon it without fear')" As his mighty bulk thrust against the wooden post, it cracked ominously. It was fortunate that the king is not superstitious, for the post represented England in his metaphor.

The European merchants had a well-founded grievance in their complaints against the premier, my old colleague Sateki. It was not that he was obstinate, or that he was ignorant, though I was assured that the most stubborn Carolina mule might resent being mentioned in the same breath with the Prime Minister; it was that he was no longer incorruptible. There were slanderous stories of cases of merchandise delivered at his door that had never been paid for over the counter, but, putting these aside, there was the fact that a certain Semitic firm, not long established in the group, had the ear of the Cabinet, imported most of the stores required by the government, and could oblige its friends and harass its enemies with an ease that would have been impossible if the Cabinet had been impartial. When I brought these matters to the notice of the king he said, "Without doubt Sateki is very unpopular; you see, he is like Mr. Joseph Chamberlain." Perhaps my face betrayed surprise, for he hastened to add, "Of course, I do not mean that he is as able as Mr. Chamberlain, or as eloquent; what I mean is that, like Mr. Chamberlain, Sateki says just what is in his mind without thinking, and seldom opens his lips to speak without hurting somebody's feelings." Perhaps I should add that His Majesty's only English journal is the *Review of Reviews*.

CHAPTER XV

FAREWELL

WE had now been in Tonga for six weeks, and still the chiefs tarried. But the arrival of the monthly steamer from New Zealand met the difficulty. Through the kindly offices of my friend Captain Crawshaw, who had frequently done good service for the British Government in similar emergencies, the whole of the rank and fashion of the Friendly Islands was landed on Nukualofa wharf within the week, and on May 17th we rode to the palace to meet the House of Lords assembled in council. I found them sitting in the dining-room on rows of chairs as at a charity meeting. The king presided, seated on his throne at a table, and I was provided with a chair on his left. Some of the nobles arrived heated and late; they explained to me afterwards that they had been turned back by the sentry at the doors, and told to go home and don black coats, which accounted for the funereal aspect of the meeting. The only absentees were bed-ridden; even poor old blind Tungi had been wheeled to the palace in his bath-chair. Among the new arrivals by the steamer was Mateialona, the most intelligent and enlightened of all the chiefs. The son of an elder brother of the king's mother, he would have had an earlier claim to the throne but for the bar sinister: the influence that he would have derived from his birth and character has been somewhat neutralised by his loyalty to the Wesleyan Church, which made him choose exile to Fiji rather than bow the knee to the Free Church which Mr. Baker had set up. He is now Governor of Haapai, and whatever hope there may be of the regeneration of King George's Cabinet is centred in him. With his portrait before the reader it is scarcely necessary to say that he is a man of great purpose and strength of character. The proceedings were conducted with the old-world courtesy and decorum which is fast dying out in Tonga, except among the men of high degree. This is not the place to describe the intricacies of our long, but friendly contest; it is enough to say that after nightfall on the second day of debate all the main difficulties had been overcome. As it was so late, the king of his own motion proposed that we should adjourn for dinner to Dr. Maclennan's house, and sign the treaty before we separated for the night. We made a singular procession. The night was very dark, and the king's guards hastily procured lanterns to light their master, who, I believe, had not left the compound of his palace to pay such a visit since his marriage. We overtook Tungi's bath-chair in the darkness; I believe that the king would have avoided the meeting if he had been alone, for his relations with the blind chief were anything but cordial; but the stately manners of Tongan chiefs came to his aid, and their complimentary speeches would have been thought unsparing for a friendship of many years' standing. "Farewell, Wiliame," cooed the king at parting; "I will come and drink a bowl of kava with you." His Majesty must have been thinking of another and a better world.

J. MATEIALONA

COUSIN OF THE KING AND GOVERNOR OF HAAPAI

I trembled when I thought of our kind host, who had been waiting dinner for more than an hour, and was now to have two royal, hungry, and uninvited guests sprung upon him. But he bore the invasion with his usual good-nature, and set his cook to work, while Webber played the part of David to our Saul with the piano. As soon as the cloth was drawn we got to work. Guards crowded the verandahs; native secretaries sat on the floor drafting amendments, which the king produced from under the table like cards from a conjurer's hat, only to have them gently but firmly put aside. At one in the morning we were agreed on the main points, and the king, who had long been yawning, drove off in his carriage, leaving the negotiation of the minor points to Fatafehi, his father, whom he had appointed his plenipotentiary. This cleared the air, and at half-past two, the oil in the last lamp having given out, the treaty was signed by the light of a guttering candle. Then, and not till then, was it discovered that the privy seal had been left at the palace, and we had to wait until a messenger had galloped for it on horseback. Then Fatafehi and I exchanged presents, and we were free to go to bed. The thing that had astonished the king most was Webber's extraordinary power of writing correctly from dictation Tongan, of which he did not understand a word, the secret being that Tongan is written phonetically with the Italian vowels, and that, so long as the speaker indicates the divisions between the words, the task is not so difficult as it sounds.

Next day we said good-bye to our kind hosts and went on board the *Porpoise* to prepare for our departure. Having duly appointed ten o'clock on the morning of May 19th, 1900, for taking leave of the king, we landed with a guard of honour of fifty men, and visited the palace for the last time. Our reception was the same as on the occasion of our arrival. In the presence of his ministers I gave the king some wholesome advice, and he asked me to be the bearer of a letter of thanks to the Queen. On leaving the palace we took our way to the middle of the public square, where a large crowd was assembled. The guard of honour fell in behind us and the proclamation of a Protectorate was read in English and Tongan.

As the guard presented arms, the signalman on board, who was watching our proceedings through a glass, gave the word, and at the pull of a string the ship was dressed with flags from stem to stern, and the first of twenty-one guns was fired. Then we returned on board, leaving a sergeant of marines to serve copies of the proclamation upon the king, the premier, the foreign consuls, and the heads of missions. While we were getting up steam we saw flags hoisted on every flagstaff, and a number of people came on board to take leave of us. From the king came a note enclosing his letter to the Queen and thanking me for all that had been done. Of the numerous native presents the most interesting was that from my fellow-plenipotentiary, Fatafehi, who sent a curious stone celt.[12]

As the sun set Tonga was a mere cloud upon the horizon, and the *Porpoise* was plunging in a heavy westerly swell. I had seen the little kingdom in three phases—under the dictatorship of Mr. Baker in 1886, under old King George in 1891, when I was one of his ministers, and as a British Protectorate. May the Protectorate remain purely nominal for many years to come! That rests with the Tongans. If they will abstain from squabbling among themselves, keep free from debt, and govern themselves decently, there is no reason that their status should change, though the history of little states is not reassuring. The scattered group has been under one king as long as tradition runs; its people have played a notable part in the history of the Pacific as navigators, conquerors, and colonists; and I for one should be grieved if the last native state in the Pacific should pass away.

APPENDIX

TONGAN MUSIC

T HE music of the Tongans was inseparable from the dance (by which I mean the rhythmic movements of any part of the body), and it therefore esteemed rhythm before melody or harmony. There were two principal forms, the *Me'e-tu'u-baki* (dance standing up with paddles) and the *Otuhaka* (song, with gestures). Since the inculcation of English hymn-singing a third form, known as the *Lakalaka*, which is music composed by Tongans on the European model, has been introduced, and of this the Tongans are inordinately fond. Fortunately the taste of the older chiefs and the influence of the French missionaries have been strong enough to preserve the old forms intact, and both the *Me'e-tu'u-baki* and the *Otuhaka* are given on ceremonial occasions, though their ultimate decay is certain.

The specimens of Polynesian music that have found their way into the text-books are, from Mariner downward, nearly all inaccurate. Written down by untrained musicians, they have afterwards been "faked" to bring them into line with our notation, and (infamy of infamies) harmonised! The visit of a composer with time on his hands and a patient determination to record the native music faithfully, at any sacrifice of time and temper, was an opportunity not to be neglected. Soon after our arrival, therefore, we paid a visit to Mua, where the old music is most cultivated, and invited the people to entertain us with the *Lakalaka*, for we had naval officers with us, and the *Otuhaka* is strong meat for the uninitiated. At the close of the performance I sent for the leader, Finease (which is Phineas), and unfolded my proposal, which was that, for value to be received, he and a select band of musicians of the old school should come to Nukualofa and sing without ceasing until they had yielded up their treasures to the paper. Plainly they thought it a fatuous proceeding, but they consented lightly, not knowing what lay before them.

Three mornings later we were at work in the huge wooden shed which serves Dr. Maclennan as operating-room and hospital. At the further end lay two patients who had undergone serious operations on the previous afternoon; what they thought of our proceedings I do not know, but I could make a shrewd guess from the expression of the old ladies who were nursing them. Amherst Webber sat at a deal table littered with music-paper, with Phineas and three middle-aged ladies, all noted singers, sitting in a row on the floor before him. He wore a harassed air, for it soon transpired that the ladies, thinking that they knew better than he did what he wanted, were bent on running through their *répertoire* without *encore*. When I explained that they would have to sing each phrase, not twice, but perhaps forty times over, they were at first amused and afterwards distinctly bored. Webber found it impossible to take the music down phrase by phrase, because they were incapable of picking up the melody where they had left it; the only way was to make them begin each time at the beginning, and carry the score a few notes further with every repetition. Moreover, it was discovered that Phineas seldom sang the same phrase in exactly the same notes, for the melody is overlaid with innumerable turns and ornaments at the will of the singer, and these are impossible to represent in our notation. Two hours at a time being as much as writer or singer could stand with safety, the work took several days, but, thanks to the good sense of Phineas and the patience of Webber, a valuable collection was ultimately made. For the notes I am, of course, indebted to Amherst Webber.

1. THE "ME'E-TU'U-BAKI."

A good drawing of this dance is to be found in *Cook's Voyages*, and, as Mariner also has described it, I need say no more than that it is performed by men, drawn up in one line or two, who perform certain slow and stately evolutions, accompanying the music by twirling a light wooden instrument carved in the shape of a paddle. The rhythm is set by three large wooden drums, and a number of men sitting round them sing the words, which consist generally of a single phrase, endlessly reiterated. Unlike the *Otuhaka*, the *Me'e-tu'u-baki* is not contrapuntal, and, though a number of voices maintain one note while the others sing the melody, it may be said to be sung in unison. To the European ear, despite its marked character, it is indescribably monotonous, for the words have no meaning, and the phrase is repeated for twenty minutes at a stretch, without any variation except an occasional *crescendo*. The native, however, regarding it as a mere accompaniment, concentrates his attention on the dance, which, though also monotonous to our eyes, is full of ancient grace and dignity to his.

ME'E-TU'U-BAKI.
Listen

2. THE "OTUHAKA."

Though it may be performed standing, the singers of the *Otuhaka* generally sit in a single line, loaded with garlands and anointed with scented oil. The feature of the performance is the *haka,* or gesture-dance, for though the performers may be sitting, it is still a dance. Head, eyes, arms, fingers, knees, and even toes all have their part, and the precision of the gestures is extraordinary. The talent may be said to be born in every Tongan, for you may see little mites of eight years old shyly take their places at the end of the row and acquit themselves without a slip. The *Otuhaka* opens with a long and threatening solo on the drum, consisting of the same bar insistently repeated. After thirty bars or so the gesture dance begins in silence to the same monotonous accompaniment, until at last, when you have almost given up hope of anything more, the leader bursts into song, the rhythm of the drum never varying until it quickens up towards the end. All the performers sing; the leader takes the melody, and the chorus the second part, for the *Otuhaka*, which are generally of the same form, are always in two parts, and usually in rough canon. Here, too, there is an interminable repetition of the same theme until the leader gives the signal for a change by striking a higher note, and then the gestures change, the time quickens, and the chorus breaks into the *tali*, or coda, ending with a long-drawn note and a sudden dropping of the voice down the scale, like an organ when the bellows give out. The time is generally common or two-four, but in one of the examples given below the time is three-eight.

In reading these examples it is to be remembered that the leader loads his melody with turns and grace notes which are never quite the same, and which are impossible to write down, and further, that the final note always ends with the peculiar groan which I have described.

From a photograph by   *J. Martin,*
Auckland.

THE OTUHAKA

The two drummers sit in the middle of the semicircle

OTUHAKA (1) Listen

[Transcriber's note: Words taken from sheet music; song for two voices, overlapping as in a round.]

He nonu a tongi a tongi e a nonu a tongi
He nonu a tongi a tongi e
He nonu a tongi a tongi e a nonu a tongi
He nonu a tongi a tongi e
He nonu a tongi a tongi e a

[English translation by transcriber: The nonu tree to be carved. (repeat) Dancers miming carving? Tongan
hakas are done sitting down, with upper body movements only.]

OTUHAKA (2) Koe Kolo Kakala. Listen

Tau matangi tule i he Vai
   Tau matangi tule i he Vai
Tule i he Vai
Tau matangi tule i he Vai
   Tau matangi tule i he fua
Tau malu
   Tau matangi tule
Tau matangi tule i he Vai

[English translation by transciber:

We have a soft wind on the water
We have a soft wind going our way
We are safe
We have a soft wind on the water

Perhaps the motions of the dancers mimicked

rowing.]

OTUHAKA in three-eight time. Listen

From these examples it will be seen that the old Tongan scale is limited to the following notes:—

Listen

In the absence of any indication of the chord, it would be incorrect to speak of tonic or dominant, but if we assume the key to be C minor, we may say that the Tongans have no fifth, nor leading note, and that they are not enamoured of the fourth. It is not that any of these intervals are abhorrent, for, as we shall presently see, they have taken very kindly to our notation in the *Lakalaka*, where a progression of consecutive fifths seems to afford them peculiar delight. The character of their music is contrapuntal and not harmonic, though in their church music they are intensely fond of the full chord. The intonation in singing is very nasal, and though the men were easily taught to correct this fault in singing European music, the women are incorrigible. The explanation offered to me by a native lady was that opening the mouth wide while singing swelled a disfiguring vein in the throat, but I suspect the real reason to be that which prompts them to conceal a yawn behind the hand—namely, that it is indelicate to expose the inside of the mouth to public gaze.

3. THE "LAKALAKA."

The only interesting feature in the *Lakalaka* lies in the fact that it is music composed by natives under the influence of European music. It shows little talent or invention, and its more ambitious melodies and crude harmonies, however spirited the performance, pall quite as quickly as the *Otuhaka*, which has at least a weird and striking character of its own. The composer of the

Lakalaka is at once poet and dancing-master as well as composer. When the afflatus is upon him he retires to the bush, and returns with words, music, and appropriate gestures complete in his head, and an hour's practice suffices to make all the boys and girls in his village perfect in their parts. Finease Fuji was one of these, and his reputation ensured a public performance to all his compositions. Those that become popular may endure for many years. *Langa fale kakala* (build a house of flowers), for example, which is given below, is as popular a favourite now as it was when I was in Mua in 1886. The themes are boating songs, odes to Nature and to flowers, or laments, but never love-songs. I remember one very pathetic lamentation of a poet named Tubou, whose theme was a term of six months' hard labour awarded him for flirting; it attained immense popularity on account of its pathos; indeed, I think that the pathetic *Lakalaka* are the most enduring. Love-songs are called *sipi*, and they are never sung in public, being rather in the nature of sonnets to my lady's eyebrow.

Like the *Otuhaka*, the *Lakalaka* is in two parts, though the voices may divide into four parts in the final chord. They are contrapuntal in form as well as harmonic, and they are accompanied with the same kind of gesture dance as the *Otuhaka*. The singers may either sit or stand in one or two rows; if they stand, the men go through a sort of dance, while the women move their heads and arms without changing their position. The difference between the two forms lies in the scale, for the *Lakalaka* makes use of our scale both major and minor, with the exception of the leading note, which is generally omitted; the melody is more sustained, and, no drum being used in accompaniment, the rhythm is less marked.

The European music which have been the foundation of the *Lakalaka* are Wesleyan hymns, military band marches, and Mozart's Twelfth Mass, which is very well done by the students of the Wesleyan College. Most of the educated natives can read very well in the *tonic sol-fa* notation, and they have now begun to compose a kind of choral anthem for themselves, which is very much like the *Lakalaka* without the gestures. They show a great aptitude for keeping their parts, even in complicated counterpoint. That they have a strong natural turn for music is certain; it is the exception to find a native without a voice and a correct ear, and if they lack originality themselves, they have at least a very quick appreciation. I have described elsewhere[13] how the Grand March from Tännhauser took them by storm when it was first performed, albeit imperfectly, by the king's band.

LAKALAKA.

by FINEASE FUJI of MUA.
Listen

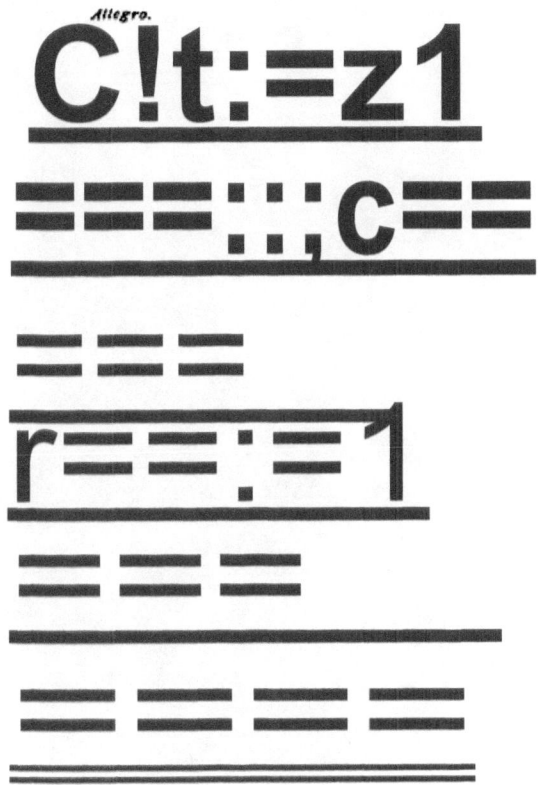

INDEX

Crawshaw, Captain. <u>211</u>

Crime, an unknown. <u>113</u>

Crime and its punishment. <u>103</u> *et seq.*

Crook, Mr.. <u>75</u>

Cruise of H.M.S. "Fawn," The. <u>80</u> (footnote)

Custom, a unique. <u>92</u>

Dance, a native. <u>119</u>, <u>120</u>

Disease, native fear of. <u>75</u>, <u>76</u>;
  introduced by whalers. <u>78</u>

Diseases of the natives. <u>133</u> *et seq.*

"Dongai," <u>100</u>

Duel, a mimic. <u>121</u>

Duff, the. <u>75</u>, <u>105</u>

Dunedin, the Bishop of. <u>162</u>

Earth, tradition of the peopling of the. <u>84</u>

Eaves-dropping. <u>208</u>

Elephantiasis, cases of. <u>176</u>

English, Mr.. <u>131</u>

Entertainment, a native. <u>117</u> *et seq.*

Erskine, Captain, visit of, to Niué. <u>77</u>

European merchants. <u>209</u>

Evil spirits, belief in. <u>99</u>

Fornander. <u>91</u>

French missionaries, the influence of. <u>218</u>

Fujipala. <u>182</u>

Futuna. <u>21</u>, <u>22</u>

Treaty, the signing of a. <u>30</u>, <u>172</u> *et seq.*; 214

Tuapa. <u>9</u>, <u>10</u>. <u>35</u> (footnote). <u>36</u>, <u>54</u>. <u>55</u>, <u>63</u>. <u>134</u>;
 cave near. <u>65</u>;
 the road to. <u>49</u>;
 the King's palace in. <u>54</u>

Tui Belehake. *See* Fatafehi

Tui Kanakubolu, death portent of the. <u>197</u>

— Tonga, the. <u>88</u>

Tuitonga, King. <u>2</u>, <u>35</u>. <u>36</u> (footnote)

Tukuaho. <u>154</u>, <u>157</u>. <u>158</u>, <u>163</u>

Tungi. <u>154</u>, <u>163</u>. <u>195</u>, <u>212</u>. <u>213</u>

Turner, Dr.. <u>75</u>-7. <u>96</u>, <u>106</u>

Tutunekai, the. <u>146</u>

Ugliness, the cult of. <u>129</u>

Unga. <u>188</u>

Utulei Point. <u>184</u>

Vavau. <u>172</u>, <u>182</u> *et seq.*;
 the native church of. <u>16</u>, <u>18</u>;
 the German coaling-station at. <u>186</u>, <u>187</u>

Victoria, Queen, letter to, from native chiefs. <u>1</u>;
 from King Tongia. <u>151</u>;
 a portrait of. <u>23</u>, <u>28</u>;
 autograph letters for. <u>150</u>;
 presents from the King of Tonga. <u>167</u>

PLYMOUTH
WILLIAM BRENDON AND SON, PRINTERS

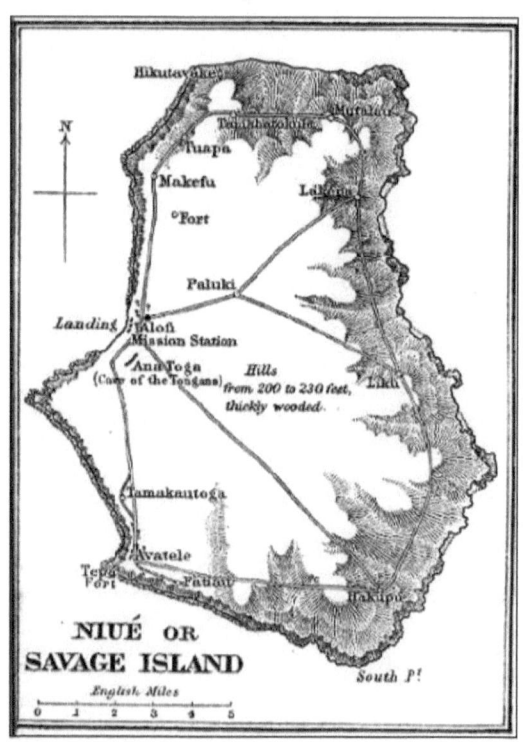

FOOTNOTES:

[1] In October, 1900, the boat that landed Lord Ranfurly for the ceremony of annexation shipped a big sea, and the captain of H.M.S. *Mildura* so re-formed the landing-place with gun cotton that a boat may now turn round in it.

[2] Here I may remark that His Majesty lacked his usual frankness, for the first recruiting vessel that called after my visit found him as active an ally as ever.

[3] The two great stones against which Tongia's last two predecessors had leaned may still be seen standing in the square before Alofi Church. Tongia chose to have the ceremony at his own village of Tuapa.

[4] The following is a list of the kings as far back as their names are recorded:—

1. Punimata of Halafualangi, who reigned at Fatuaua (died).
2. Galiaga of Pulaki (killed).
3. Patuavalu of Puato (died).
4. Pakieto of Utavavau (starved to death).

Interregnum of eighty years.

5. Tuitonga (succeeded 1876).
6. Fataäiki (succeeded 1888).

Interregnum of nearly two years.

7. Tongia (succeeded 1898).

[5] The Diversions of a Prime Minister.

[6] The *Messenger of Peace* was the most remarkable vessel that ever plied among the islands. She was built in Rarotonga, for the most part by natives who had never handled tools before. Williams killed his goats to make bellows for welding the bolts, and, when his iron ran out, he fastened his planking with wooden trenails. Cocoanut fibre stood for oakum, but there was not an ounce of pitch or paint for caulking. She was of about sixty tons burden. When she put to sea with her landsman captain, her crew of natives, who had never been to sea, and her cargo of pigs, cocoanuts, and cats, she must have been a sight to make a seaman weep.

[7] The vile anchorages of Niué are responsible for the loneliness of the Europeans. Even in these days of more or less regular steam communication among the islands the visits of ships are so rare that the Europeans have come to believe in omens foretelling their arrival. An insect settling on the dining-table is one of these, and the Mission party laughingly recalled the fact that this portent had raised their hopes two days before our arrival. Never were people so easy to entertain. It happened that the captain had some new carbons of French make to test in his searchlight, and the people took his experiments to be a display of fireworks for their amusement. The brilliant flashes, which, in the more sophisticated islands would not have drawn an European to his door, were watched with rapture, and every native who was entangled in the dazzling beam went frantic with delight.

[8] *The Cruise of H.M.S. "Fawn,"* by T. H. Hood, London, 1862.

[9] *Camping and Tramping in Malaya*, by H. Rathbone, 1898.

[10] The Mission returns put the total population at 19,968: Tongatabu, 8,454; Haapai, 5,087; Vavau, 4,589; Niuatobutabu, 710; Niuafoou, 1,128. The males exceed the females by 454, or 2.2 per cent., and the adults outnumber the children.

[11] *Mariner's Account of the Tonga Islands.* By John Martin, M.D.

[12] This celt measures 9½ inches long by 3-3/8 inches wide in the broadest part, made

of an olive-green stone with grey longitudinal veins, and beautifully polished. It was clear that it had come from another part of the Pacific, for the Tongan celts are wedge-shaped, angular, and roughly made. Sir William Macgregor, who saw it on my return to England, at once pronounced it to be from New Guinea, and identified the stone as belonging to the quarry that he had discovered in Woodlark Island. All that Fatafehi could say was that it had been for generations in his family, and if this was true, the celt might be used as evidence of a Tongan migration from the west, for there were no whalers or sandalwooders before 1790; but there have been Tongan teachers working in New Guinea, and he may have been mistaken about its age.

_[13]_   _The Diversions of a Prime Minister._

www.ingramcontent.com/pod-product-compliance
Lightning Source LLC
Chambersburg PA
CBHW021233020726
47498CB00008B/2822